UNDER A DARK SUN

UNDER A DARK SUN

Jessica Mann

Chivers Press • Thorndike Press
Bath, England   Thorndike, Maine USA

This Large Print edition is published by Chivers Press, England, and by Thorndike Press, USA.

Published in 2001 in the U.K. by arrangement with Constable & Robinson Ltd.

Published in 2001 in the U.S. by arrangement with Lavinia Trevor Literary Agency.

U.K. Hardcover   ISBN 0–7540–4422–X   (Chivers Large Print)
U.K. Softcover   ISBN 0–7540–4423–8   (Camden Large Print)
U.S. Softcover   ISBN 0–7862–3221–8   (General Series Edition)

The text of this Large Print edition is unabridged.
Other aspects of the book may vary from the original edition.

Set in 16 pt. New Times Roman.

Printed in Great Britain on acid-free paper.

British Library Cataloguing in Publication Data available

Library of Congress Cataloging-in-Publication Data

Mann, Jessica.
    Under a dark sun / Jessica Mann.
        p.   cm.
    ISBN 0–7862–3221–8 (lg. print : sc : alk. paper)
    1. Inheritance and succession—Fiction. 2. Executors and administrators—Fiction. 3. Cornwall (England : County)—Fiction. 4. London (England)—Fiction. 5. Large type books. I. Title.
    PR6063.A374 U54 2001
    823'.914—dc21   00–068291

CHAPTER ONE

Addison Road, Holland Park, W14. Behind an in-and-out drive, a beautifully refurbished and fitted house c. 6500 sq ft with a south-west facing garden c. 100 ft x 60ft. 6 bedrooms, with en-suite bathrooms, shower room, large drawing-room, conservatory, dining-room, study, office, kitchen, staff flat, covered heated pool, double garage, parking. Freehold. Offers in the region of £6 million. Sold for over £8 million. (House agent's advertisement, autumn 1998)

Stopping her cab on Holland Park Avenue, Marguerite decides to walk the rest of the way. A tall, lithe woman, from behind she looks younger than her age, which is fifty-five. In full face deeply lined, tanned skin and hooded blue eyes are revealed, with bleached and gleaming hair tied back in a knot of velvet on her neck. Her clothes are discreet and ageless, a black roll-neck sweater over velvet jeans, loafers with snaffles, a straight camel hair coat, a dévoré scarf, no jewellery. She's thought very carefully about what to wear today.

As her heels click along the pavement Marguerite suddenly notices that she is subconsciously trying not to step on the lines, like a child keeping monsters at bay, and makes herself plant her feet across two paving stones. There have been monsters here, robbers and stalkers and at least one murderer, but now Marguerite, two hundred yards in, thinks the street looks subdued and polished up, with all its predators, human, animal or mythical, firmly kept at bay.

Addison Road has long since been designated as a conservation area, the district is convenient for the City to the east and the airports to south and west, few detached houses in their own grounds still stand in the capital, and the consequence is that these bourgeois homes built for Victorian merchants are now among the most valuable properties in London. One of them has recently been sold for eight million pounds.

Even the public highway proclaims the area's wealth. Cars parked at the kerb are large and gleaming, the road protected from use as a north-south rat run by chicanes and speed humps, and the pavements regularly cleaned, though even in February there are still some of last year's leaves to fall from the London plane trees. Do the kids who live here now, seldom allowed out without a grown-up, still shuffle their feet through the dusty russet piles before mechanical sweepers take them away? For there are no aromatic bonfires any more; this has been a smokeless zone for forty years.

In 1944 this block was consumed with smoke, flames and dust, a patch out of hell. A

2

flying-bomb had fallen in the middle of the night, a whole row of houses blazed till dawn and smouldered for three days before the bodies, four of them, could be taken from the ruins. The hole in the ground, quickly overgrown with brambles and willow herb, was later turned into a piggery where the farmer lived on site in a hut built out of scrap metal. The neighbours complained for years of the rustic stink, even though meat rationing made them desperate for supplies of bacon and pork. In the sixties a developer bought the land and built an estate of yellow-brick flats and houses. Marguerite observes that they have faded into acceptability, and most are prettified with swathes of wistaria or enhanced by decorative gables, porches and balconies.

She sees that there is a police presence down one of the estate's private roads and makes a little detour. Red and white tape is flapping in the wind. There's a raw excavation in someone's back garden, untouched since the autumn when, as Marguerite had read, workmen digging a hole in a back garden for a swimming pool came upon a skeleton. It was assumed to be that of another nameless bomb victim. The police public relations department told the local paper that attempts would be made to identify it further through scientific analysis of the remains and historical research into records of those missing after air-raids.

South of the one-time bomb site, rows of

3

matching, double-fronted nineteenth-century villas stand on either side of the road, each surrounded by private grounds, all cream-painted with black woodwork and burglar-proof electric gates.

Number 441, 443, 445 . . . Here it is. The only house still in need of a lick of paint, still lacking landscaping and security fencing and drive resurfacing and all the other expensive prinking its neighbours have long since received. Scrawny privet hedges flank a weedy path. The garden wall of dingy London bricks is suffocated by ivy. A dead cherry tree leans dangerously over the area steps beside a leggy rose, to which one withered yellow flower still clings. The gate is hanging off its hinges. A woman's bike is chained to the rusty fence, paint is peeling from the walls and one could only guess that the front door had once been green.

A pole topped by a 'For Sale' placard is planted in the front garden. Marguerite pauses by the gate and reads it. Then, in no hurry, relishing the moment, she scans the frontage, counts the windows, two tall sashes flanking the central door, one, two, three symmetrical sashes on the upper floor and three smaller windows behind a balustrade at the top. *Three floors and a basement kitchen. Driveway, garage and outbuildings. Gardens front and back. Conservatory. Potential for swimming pool.* She fingers the estate agents' particulars folded into her pocket. *A desirable residence, some modernisation required. Price on application, viewing by appointment only.*

Marguerite knows the asking price and has no appointment, but she pushes the gate wide and treads deliberately along the slimy path and up the six shallow steps to the door. The brass bell is deeply tarnished. Putting her shinily tipped forefinger on the button, she presses it long and hard.

CHAPTER TWO

For Hilly James this was a tour like any other, except for the fact that Ari, the lecturer, was really fanciable, which was not a detail she could include in her returns to the travel company. She completed the forms as usual, with a fresh sheet fastened to the clipboard each morning and spaces for all the details of time taken at each attraction; the relative efficiency, or otherwise, of the local agents; the ailments and complaints of the pax. She'd admitted to Ari, the only other person under forty, the only man who was neither bald nor grey, that remembering the individual members of the party would be quite another matter. If one escorted twenty groups a year all over the world, in Peru one week and Petra the next, singling out all the individual punters in that trip from a mish-mash of muddled memories was expecting rather too much. 'You're different though,' she'd added, fixing her gaze on his tanned, thin features. He took in the softness of her pink skin, her generous bosom, her melting eyes and English diffidence, and responded with an impersonal, discouraging dip of the chin.

The tour went from north to south, Manchuria downwards through China to finish up in Hong Kong. The programme had sounded sensible to Mr Feuerstein, who had had the idea in the first place and gathered the participants via his Internet news group, but Hilly said she was going to tell the company that it was a bit of a downer to start on a low note. Ari did not care. The punters, he said, could like it or lump it, quoting words he'd once read in some otherwise long-forgotten story about British schoolboys.

By day two some of the travellers were letting their disenchantment show, especially those who had come along with their partners for the ride, promising themselves visits to China's art and monuments, which, in Manchuria, were in limited supply. On first sight in the check-in queue at Heathrow Mr Feuerstein had seemed younger than expected, for someone whose passport said he'd been born in 1920. He was the only orthodox member of the party, wearing a skull cap and a straggling beard and refusing the non-kosher food on the long flight, which was probably why it had exhausted him. He also proved to be quite deaf, so he was not much help with soothing his companions. Ari took no notice of snide remarks, which passed him by as though he too could not hear them, and, being paid to listen, Hilly wasn't allowed to answer back. Anyone else would have been quite sharp with Mrs Harpner, a pink matron from Florida who had been appalled by her very first sight of the teeming masses and her very first whiff of China's universal smell. Mr 'Call-Me-Chuck' Harpner, who addressed his wife as 'Mother', had told her, many times, in public and very loudly, that she shouldn't have come, nobody made her come, he'd never wanted her to come in the first place and if she didn't like it that was her own tough shit. She didn't like it; not the autumn colours in the virgin forest or the jagged rocky peaks of the nature reserve at Changbai, nor Mirror Lake, nor the Lake of Heaven or its neighbouring waterfall and wealth of legends, and specially not the hot springs bath house, where the local ladies had gathered round to watch her squat in the rest-room's doorless cubicle.

The other pax—as travel professionals call passengers—faded into acceptability beside the whining Mrs Harpner, though even after the twenty-one days Ari never did memorise their names. Hilly learnt them quickly and forgot them with equal facility after the trip was over.

A pretty dull lot, she'd indiscreetly remarked one evening, late, in her utilitarian hotel room, pouring water from the wicker-encased vacuum jug on to the coffee granules she had prudently brought along. Ari stood restlessly by the sealed window, his dark floppy hair and derisive mouth intermittently illuminated by a flashing pink neon sign outside. He always wore the same clothes, a torn green sweater, desert boots and tattered jeans, with a padded jacket out of doors but no other variation. Depending on her state of mind, Hilly thought he smelled sexy or dirty. The trouble was that no matter how much of her duty-free scotch she poured down his throat, Ari retained a reserve she seemed unable to breach. She was afraid he included her in the category of 'a dull lot'. But all he said was that the punters had paid up, hadn't they? In other, unspoken words, they had paid enough to cover his free trip.

Mr Feuerstein had insisted on doing everything properly so it was an expensive trip for the paying passengers. A pair of sisters from Burnley who visibly shrank on their neurotic regime of mineral water and boiled rice. Four married couples, with home addresses in Washington, Arizona, Surbiton and Rome. They had eight Burberry macintoshes, six navy blue blazers and three cases of diarrhoea and vomiting between them. Four singletons, three women and Mr Feuerstein, who seemed to be living on the contents of his suitcase, two weeks' supply of dried food and muesli bars. And Ari.

Hilly had taken charge of all the passports on the flight out, so she knew that Ari was thirty, had a home address in Jerusalem, and temporary work permits stamped in for the United States and the United Kingdom. He was a visiting professor at one of the New York colleges and something he'd let slip in her hearing had told Hilly that he'd been a kibbutznik from an Israeli collective farm until he left for college.

Sloane Ranger Hilly, widely, if superficially, travelled, was realistic about her own limited education, appearance and attractions. She knew it was her very ordinariness that made her good at the mixture of nannying and non-committal flirting which the job entailed. But as far as Ari was concerned, she was well aware she hadn't a hope. It would be quite a comfort if he turned out to be gay.

Mr Feuerstein had found Ari through his Internet news group too; its subject was the Jewish diaspora, and its members had previously visited Brazil, South Africa and the island of Madagascar which had been proposed as a Jewish national home in the 1920s. For China they needed a guide who was knowledgeable about Sino-Judaica, a subject Ari had been particularly interested in because his father, like Mr Feuerstein's, had been born in Manchuria, both families having left Russia in 1917 and settled along with White Russsian exiles in and around Harbin. There had once been a sizeable community of Jewish settlers in North China.

Mr Feuerstein's parents had moved away from Manchuria before he was born but his grandparents had stayed there, and died in Pingfan. He led the men of the party in memorial prayers when the party reached the town, watched curiously by a gathering circle of local people.

Later everyone assembled in a bleak conference room in the hotel's basement for Ari's talk. It was a stuffy, dust-impregnated space furnished with dozens of gilt chairs and colour photocopies of embroidered textiles.

Ari spoke of the Japanese invasion of Manchuria in 1931. The red sun of the imperial flag flew all over the country. The Japanese set up a puppet state whose head, in name only, was the Last Emperor of China. 'You folks all seen the movie?' Yes, they had, they knew about Pu Yi.

'OK, listen up,' Ari began. Hilly loved his accent, mildly East Coast American with an undertone of his more liquid, throaty native language.

'This is what the Japs did in Pingfan. A one horse dump. Was then, still is, right?' Ari's audience had lunched off grey dumplings in a

10

diner from hell with cauldrons bubbling on an open fire and offal bloodying the dirt floor. They had been shown to grimy cells in a bleak hotel with endless concrete corridors where the telephones did not work and the lavatories did not flush until Hilly came and did efficient things to the cisterns with her travelling tool kit. The plumbing seemed to have been installed by workmen who had seen pictures of bathroom fixtures but did not understand their function.

They all nodded in whole-hearted agreement. Pingfan was indeed a dump.

An infamous dump.

The Japanese had based an army division there. Unit 751. Its full name was the Epidemic Prevention and Water Supply Unit.

The unit had been formed in 1936. It had a single, specific function: to carry out research into bacterial warfare. The boss was a surgeon, a fanatical Japanese nationalist called Dr Shiro Ishii. They made him a full general later on. Ishii's sidekick was Dr Saburo Okuda and under them there were hundreds of other doctors, scientists and technicians. They produced anthrax, dysentery, typhoid, cholera and bubonic plague germs, enough lethal microbes to wipe out the world several times over. They provided disease bombs to test in raids on China.

Drs Ishii and Okuda developed techniques for experimenting on human guinea-pigs. They

11

called them marutas, which means logs. To discover how much lethal bacteria would be necessary to create epidemics, they gave three thousand of these human logs bubonic plague and other diseases, all of them slowly or, if they were lucky, quickly lethal.

This was the point at which Mrs Harpner interrupted, crying, 'That's so gross, I don't need to hear this.'

It was her husband who made the crushing reply. 'You do too. If people endured it the least we can do is know what happened.'

Ari went on, his voice level and icy. 'Other victims were shot in ballistics tests or frozen to death to investigate frostbite. Some were electrocuted, others boiled alive or exposed to lethal radiation or vivisected.'

A voice said the word 'Mengele.'

'An oriental Mengele, but he had infinitely more victims, ten times as many people suffered under Ishii,' Ari said. 'But he and Mengele were committing the same crimes. Ishii conducted experiments to determine the differential reactions of various races to disease.'

'Our people,' Mr Feuerstein murmured. His lips went on moving silently. He might have been praying.

'Jews and Chinese, and after Japan came into the war, British and Commonwealth prisoners-of-war as well. And GIs.'

There were exclamations then, from the

12

Americans in the party. A sombre silence followed, until a woman whispered, 'Did they all die? Every one of them?'

Ari said, 'Every single one.'

'No survivors,' one of the men murmured. His cheeks were wet. Ari went on:

'At the end of the war, any Pingfan victims still surviving were gassed or poisoned and the facilities destroyed. And as well, they released the plague-ridden rats.'

'Ishii must have been in the war crimes trials,' Harpner said.

'If only,' Mr Feuerstein breathed.

Ari said, 'The hell he was. Western scientists were just salivating at the prospect of getting the Japs' research results and the American government granted Ishii and Okuda and their team immunity from prosecution and then, you guessed it, they invited those sons of bitches into the US of A.'

'Why haven't we ever heard of this?' one of the men asked.

'Yes, why?' said another. 'If all this is true these atrocities would be as well known, documented in as much detail, as what happened in the concentration camps.'

'The American government decided to keep it all secret,' Ari said bitterly.

'They couldn't, it's not possible!'

'But it's true,' Feuerstein said. 'The Wiesenthal Foundation confirms it all, you can find the information on the Web. But nothing

13

came out at all till the 1980s.'

Ari said, 'Even then, when people asked for the documents under the Freedom of Information Act—interrogation records and so on—the whole lot had been destroyed when there was a fire at the St Louis archive. Or so it was alleged.'

'Logs,' one of the women murmured. 'How could they?'

Ari replied, 'They aren't even ashamed of it. There's a veteran of Unit 751, lives in a cosy villa outside Kobe, organises reunions with his mates. He insists he never took part in experiments on humans because his victims weren't human. They were already dead. Dead wood. Logs.'

A man said, 'Y'know, I have a feeling the US of A made its own germ bombs during the war.'

'Too right. Anthrax and botulin, both,' Ari said.

'Our own country! This is a perversion of science,' said the Washington wife, and her husband replied:

'Don't forget how ingenious our scientists are. Remember the anti-civilian personnel bombs in Vietnam, fragmentation bombs with the sharp pieces made of plastic to stop X-rays finding them for doctors to remove.'

'Only in America,' she said sadly.

'At least in World War II the allies had good reason to think Germany was about to use biological weapons,' Harpner said, and one of the blazered Englishmen added quietly:

'We did anthrax research too—it's no secret that they tested it on the island of Gruinard in the Hebrides. Nobody can ever go there again, it was poisoned for ever.' Cohen, Hilly told herself. That was Mr Cohen, whom she could only distinguish from Mr Simpson by alliteration. Curly hair Cohen, Straight Simpson. Mrs Cohen had gone sweatily red and was fanning her face with the itinerary.

'The British would never do such a thing!' she said firmly, but Mr Feuerstein answered her, in a weak, accepting tone:

'But it is clear, we all understand it now, in this century we have been taught that good men must do evil.'

Mr Cohen explained. 'The thing is, you see, you've got to find an antidote just in case the enemy use those weapons, and to do that you'd have to make the poison first. To understand it, you know? So our side had no choice. How the hell else were we ever going to defend ourselves?'

From the *Kensington and Chelsea Chronicle*, 27 February 1999

Murder probe in Royal Borough

Police have revealed that they are treating the discovery of a skeleton in Kensington as a murder investigation. The skeleton, unearthed when a patio was excavated to make a swimming pool at the Addison Road home of media tycoon Jean-Yves Chapelier, has undergone lab tests which reveal lesions consistent with blows from a blunt instrument. Previously thought to be a victim of the bomb which demolished eight properties in 1944, the skeleton is that of a middle-aged male, probably of oriental origin.

CHAPTER THREE

Someone had to sort through my aunt's junk (remains? trash? waste?) and it had become obvious in the last few weeks that it would have to be me because her heirs couldn't face it. They were her daughters (and of course Bertram's) and Katie and Christina couldn't say or hear their father's name without hysteria.

The story had gone off the boil by now, but the newspapers telling it were still lying round, folded open on the hall chair at the relevant pages. On the day the story broke it had been in full frontal headlines. *Nobel prize winner a spy*, one proclaimed. *Queen's scientist was Cambridge traitor*, was another variation. *A new book on the spies who betrayed Britain to the Soviets during the Cold War will reveal that Professor Sir Bertram Kittermaster who died in 1997 betrayed scientific and defence secrets about germ warfare via his old college friends Kim Philby and Anthony Blunt.* And so on.

The new book referred to was torn to shreds by knowledgeable critics and the scientific establishment leapt to the defence of the old man so the story died away quickly because it didn't contain any evidence whatever. The notion didn't seem to have sprung from anything more than the fact that

Bertram had overlapped with Philby, Blunt and Co. at Trinity College, Cambridge, and, as I told the girls, the number must run into double figures, of the old gentlemen who'd been similarly fingered in the last few years and quickly forgotten. I tried to persuade them it was the price of fame—for Bertram had been very famous. But mud does stick. And it's not pleasant to have your father accused of treachery. Of course it was nonsense. I for one actually found it laughable rather than tragic to think of Sir Bertram Kittermaster, CH, OM etc etc, in the role of a spy.

At least there weren't any reporters hanging round the house any more, though I'd been suspicious of two people who'd come to look at it when it was first advertised and had now told the agents to require a bank guarantee before showing prospective purchasers round. Meanwhile, we had to move everything out.

I realised that Elena hadn't thrown anything away for decades, saving up milk bills, Christmas cards or laundry lists as though some future biographer would be thrilled to find them. Her husband's working papers had been sold to an American university and maybe Elena hoped that her own domestic trivia would prove valuable too. We'd all had copies of a letter from a man signing himself M. Foster PhD, who had been commissioned to write a history of the Kittermaster family. I'd had nothing to do with that project, having

18

been told about it by my cousin Gayle after it was too late to stop it. I would have, if I could. Even before she died Elena had been worried by researchers who had been sniffing round on Bertram's traces in the sixteen months after his death and before hers. Luckily by the time those tabloid slurs were published she'd been past noticing.

As Elena's executor, it was up to me to decide if her stuff ought to be saved for Gayle's researcher or anyone else to see because Katie and Christina couldn't bring themselves either to get rid of a single scrap of their mother's papers, or to commit themselves to keeping them. So I'd had to spend the last two days doing it myself, first deciphering and then binning most of the contents of cupboards, desks, drawers and a stash of damp cardboard cartons piled in front of the wine bins in Uncle Bertram's once-famous cellar.

By now I'd reached the attic, a long, dim, raftered area which could have been used as the set of a televised ghost story. Like the rest of the house, it retained the residual smell of the tobacco with which it had, for decades, been impregnated. In one corner a dead dolls' house, in another that invariably sinister prop, the dressmaker's body form; a stack of ancient suitcases, all far too heavy to use, in sturdy brown leather, speckled with mould and still labelled with the names of distant hotels. Most

19

were empty. One was full of baby-clothes, hand-knitted lacy jackets and embroidered gowns all reeking of mothballs. Could I be bothered to drag them along to sell to a stall-holder in the Portobello market? Frankly, I thought, no.

I went through a case full of gloves, kid, suede, leather, long, short, buttoned or cuffed, another money spinner for an antiques shop, where these relics of a different style of female might seem charming and desirable. Here and now I found them creepy, like flaccid amputated hands. Shuddering, I snapped the case closed.

I could see another bag, canvas with leather trim, at the back of the pile of cases, shoved in behind the hot tank. It contained men's clothes. I wouldn't have fancied investigating with bare fingers, fingers which, my ex-husband used to complain, I never liked getting dirty, but protected by rubber gloves I checked the uncrumpled fabric of a dark grey suit made of an artificially creaseless cloth, a Brooks Brothers shirt and underwear, all shoved in on top of neatly folded pyjamas and another shirt and set of vest and pants. The underclothes bore the kind of indelible laundry marks that enabled the classic detectives to identify unknown corpses and the shirts and pyjamas were made out of that, by now obsolete, sweaty nylon of the very early drip-dries. A zipped washbag in hard, cracked leather contained a hairbrush, toothbrush and cut-throat razor, all with horn handles, a little shaving brush and bowl and some tooth powder. I felt in the coat pockets. An Underground map of London dating from a time before the Victoria or Jubilee lines were built, a small oblong pink ticket which I recognised as the kind used on London buses back when conductors were called clippies and I was a small child on a day trip to the dentist and pantomime. These were American clothes, presumably bought by Bertram on one of his transatlantic trips in the days of British clothes rationing. Another one for the skip, I thought, making myself return to the duty on hand, examining the endless, dismal (discouraging? disheartening? sad?) documents, the dross that a long life boiled down to.

I could quite see why the girls didn't want to make these repeated decisions about ephemera and memorabilia (unmemorabilia? Why isn't there an exact word for things that need forgetting?) that seemed as suddenly dead as Elena herself, who had been lively, argumentative and demanding one evening and the next morning silent and shrunken, a small shape in the big, high bed. It's not that it was exactly shocking given that Elena was old and ill, but we hadn't expected it just yet or so suddenly. 'An easy death,' Christina expertly remarked, drawing the sheet up over the empty face. Katie, who went in for romanticising, murmured, 'She ceased upon the midnight without pain.' Dr Al Masri said he would miss her but was glad she'd been spared pain he couldn't relieve, said he would go downstairs to write out the certificate and added, 'God is merciful.'

'Yes indeed,' both girls responded, all the more ardent, I sourly thought, in the knowledge of the material benefits they would now inherit. I seemed the sorriest. Not only was I going to miss Elena, but also, having been made her executor, I had to manage and wind up the estate.

There's something infinitely dispiriting about letters and cards that must have been pretty pointless even when they were written, a waste of Planet Earth's raw materials. I realised there was very little here that Mr Foster or anyone else could ever want to use except possibly for the contents of one large ringbound exercise book. Unfortunately I couldn't read a single word, since Elena's handwriting was notoriously inscrutable and, even more problematically, it was written in her native language. I don't know any Hungarian and nor do Katie and Christina. Elena once told me she'd decided to remake herself as an Englishwoman when, having lost every relation she had in the world, she arrived as a refugee in 1956. 'I abjured my former home', she said. After she married Bertram

Elena spent a fortune on elocution lessons, determined to eliminate any foreign accent— as she very nearly did; one detected it only on the telephone.

The only comprehensible line in this little notebook was the date at the beginning, 31.12.57. New Year's Eve, the year she and Bertram were married. I looked dubiously at the closely written pages. If Elena had relaxed her rule to write this in Hungarian, the contents could be secret indeed. Might she have written about her love affairs? Or something even more secret? I put the book aside to think about later.

Before throwing them away I scanned engraved invitations, printed change of address cards, birth and death announcements, handwritten notes agreeing to attend or saying it was lovely to have attended parties, holiday postcards. Some included the classic phrases *X marks the spot* and *Wish you were here.* One bundle, held together in an elastic band, contained a series of cards addressed to Bertram, pictures of Mont Blanc or K2 or other less recognisable mountains, written in a minuscule cursive and signed with an indecipherable squiggle, with equally time-honoured messages: *Keep the home fires burning* and *Long time no see* or *Better late than never.* There were countless photographs and snapshots, apart from those stuck into about thirty albums which Christina and Katie had

23

already rescued. One box contained yellowing newspaper cuttings, all on random subjects. If Elena's daughters didn't want to save any of it, I couldn't see the point in doing so either.

I had just tied up the final plastic sack of discarded papers when the doorbell rang.

One of 'the girls' could perfectly well have answered the door, but I guessed they wouldn't and neither did. At the second ring I took off my apron, washed my hands, glanced in the mirror. I like to look tidy, though don't hope for more than that, never having been beautiful. I have neat little features, round hazel eyes, clear skin and naturally dark eyebrows and lashes. I don't wear make-up so only needed to wipe a smudge off my forehead and smooth my hair back behind my ears.

By the time I got down three flights, someone was leaning on the bell. The shrill monotone echoed off the bare walls and hard tiled floor of the denuded house, but broke off as I approached the door. A tall silhouette could be seen through the glass panel and I had my usual moment of optimism—lunatic, as I was perfectly well aware, as well as shaming, pointless, and increasingly so with every passing year. All the same the thought sprang into my mind. Might this be *it*? Could this be *he*?

One didn't open the front door to strangers in London these days. I called, 'Who is it?'

'It's Mrs Lang,' someone said in a deep,

24

smooth voice.

I didn't know the name, so put the chain on and pulled the door open six inches. A mature, immaculate woman stood there. I was about to tell her it was 'viewing by appointment only' when she said, 'Well now, is this Katarina or Christina?'

'No, sorry, wait while I just . . .' I closed the door to release the chain and then opened it wide. 'I'll go and get them, who shall I say . . . ?'

She seemed to hesitate on the threshold before stepping up and placing—no, *planting*—her feet on to the patterned tiles of the outer lobby. Then she walked forward, past me and through the inner doorway, with a kind of cautious deliberation.

'Just a minute, you can't . . .' I began.

She stationed herself in the middle of the entrance hall under the unshaded light bulb and beside the only chair left there, on which lay the newspapers, already yellowing at the edges, full of the story about Bertram and treachery. She glanced at them, said, 'So much for the great man, huh?' and looked round with unmasked curiosity, up the wide staircase, through the open doors of the unfurnished morning room on one side, the dining-room on the other and along the bare-boarded back passage. There was such an air of concentrated self-possession about her that I actually hesitated to interrupt, but eventually said, 'Look, I don't know what you want, if you'll just tell me what this is about. . .'

Mrs Lang turned to look at me. In a languid, mid-Atlantic drawl she said, 'Of course, you're quite a bit older, you can't be one of the girls, I see that now.'

A bad start. I'm not really all that much older than Katie and Christina and, in any case, a gap of a few years dwindles when you're all middle-aged.

'Who are you?' she asked.

'My name's Victoria Merton—' I began, but she went on as though she hadn't heard.

'And what's going on here, where is everything?'

I said, 'The house is on the market so some furniture's gone to the saleroom and we're clearing up for the removers.'

'Where is everything? Where's the antiques and water-colours and the cabinet of curiosities?' I hesitated and she said impatiently, 'Oh come on, you know what I mean, the red lacquer case of jade.'

'As far as I know my aunt sold some of the good stuff a while ago, but I don't understand why you—'

'I suppose you're helping the family out, are you?'

'I'm the executor of Lady Kittermaster's— my aunt's estate. I'm sorry, perhaps you didn't know? She died last October.'

'So the newspapers said.' She waved at those on the chair. 'That's why I'm here.'

'Sorry, who did you say?'

'I'm Marguerite Lang, Mrs Justin Lang.'

'How d'you do?' I said, holding out my hand.

After a moment's hesitation she shook it languidly and said, 'Don't you know who I am?'

'I'm afraid I don't, but let me go and find the others, if you wouldn't mind just waiting down here, I think Christina must still be looking at the old clothes, trunkfuls of them, you wouldn't believe what a lot of stuff got saved and stored over the years.' Why was I making excuses to this arrogant stranger? There was something about her that made me gabble, which I don't usually do. 'I expect Katie's in the kitchen, I'll go and find her. If you wouldn't mind just staying here a moment?' But she wasn't listening to me.

'I'll wait in the drawing-room,' Mrs Lang said, moving towards the staircase.

'But . . .' I began, and abandoned my protest unvoiced. I ran/escaped/scuttled down the narrow stairs at the back of the house to the kitchen. We hadn't even made a start on clearing that out yet, a nightmare task in store for us. The walls were still hung with copper pans, all verdigris green but none the less saleable for that, and the dresser was still laden with multi-coloured, miscellaneous china, the relics of several tea sets and dinner services. Why ever hadn't I insisted, even

27

against Katie and Christina's will, on getting professionals in to do the dirty work, I wondered again, an ache in the small of the back reminding me of the discrepancy between the hard, dreary labour and the healthy bank account that could have paid someone else to do it.

Katie had chosen to spend the day cooking. Standing at the table sieving flour, her flowing, layered clothes protected by a striped apron and with her hair under a white cloth knotted behind her head, she was in a new disguise, this time as a central European peasant, and still role-playing said, 'I know it's too soon but I thought I'd make an Easter beigli, like Mother always used to.'

I could, if I'd cared, have read a whole new fantasy into those words, just as you can read my own obsessions into my need always to find precisely the exact/right/apposite word.

My own vocation has not changed since I studied English Language and Literature for A Level, and then at Cambridge. I've always loved words and manipulating the language. Katie, however, has spent her life assuming and later discarding experimental personae, whole-hearted every time and genuinely mystified if anyone suggested she was play-acting as she threw herself into the successive roles, among others, of a sharp-suited business woman—that was during a brief and disastrous partnership in an interior design business—or, when she was going out with a famously randy poet, of a cross between his muse and a whore with a heart of gold. She'd most recently been, and presumably still was, a seer. Of course that would not be incompatible with this new image. The Hungarian gypsy, clairvoyant Katie.

Fortune telling, reading palms, handwriting and astrology had been the longest-lasting of Katie's enthusiasms, an inspired choice by someone whose chief aim for most of the forty-two years of her life had always been to make an impression, any impression, on her father. Nothing could have been better calculated to infuriate the Nobel prize-winning scientist Professor Sir Bertram Kittermaster, than for one of his women to fall for fashionable New Age pseudo-science. Katie's new 'profession' had made the pages of a gossip magazine and at least one newspaper— which led to her getting her own column in the Argus. The family felt, I heard, an unholy glee at repeating what Uncle Bertram had said the first time he saw his name above newspaper star-sign predictions. If Katie Kittermaster's predictions did nothing else, at least they hit pay dirt in making her father take some notice of her.

I said, 'Katie, there's a visitor.'

'But the viewing's only by appointment, didn't you say?'

'It's someone called Lang, Mrs Marguerite

Lang.'

'Tell her to ring the agents, she can't just come here and—'

'I don't think she's a house hunter.'

'One of my clients? Tell her to ring first. She ought to have learnt that by now, I'm always very firm about it.'

'But I think she knows the family, you'd really better come and see her.'

'I can't leave this now.' Katie scooped a well in the pile of flour and began to pour into it some liquid from a little jug. 'This is a very delicate operation, you know, Vicky, so find Christina, why don't you, she's somewhere about the place.' Without moving from the table, Katie suddenly let out an ear-splitting yell. 'Chris!' Then she added more quietly, 'Actually, I forgot, she's gone to the hospice, there was a phone call about one of her cases.'

'Oh dear,' I said inadequately I didn't like to think about Christina's work. In private she described herself as 'the midwife to death'. She nursed dying people in a hospice.

I was trying to persuade Katie to leave her cooking—who in this house was going to eat a rich, nut-stuffed, spicy Central European cake anyway?—and come upstairs, when Mrs Lang came down herself. Standing by the kitchen door she wrinkled her nose—the room smelt of lemon zest, cinnamon, cloves and damp—and rested her gaze on the old-fashioned appliances, the huge porcelain sink and

30

wooden draining board that must have been in situ for a century, the barred window above eye level, the rag rugs on the stone-flagged floor.

'What happened to the eight-oven Aga?' she said.

'My father had it taken out when the central heating was installed—but hang on a minute, what do you know about the old Aga? Who are you?' Katie demanded.

'I know all about this house.'

'Well, I can't think how,' Katie cried, scattering flour wildly, 'but you'd still better wait for the estate agents to show you round, we can't have—'

Mrs Lang brushed a fine white dust off her lapel with a long, brown hand. She said, 'I don't need showing, I'll take a look over the whole place in a moment.'

I began to mollify, with 'I wonder whether we shouldn't just—', but at the same moment Katie let go with:

'I don't know what the hell you think you're doing, Mrs Lang, or why you've come down here—'

'Oh, don't worry I know precisely what I'm doing, it's not a secret. Not at all. The fact is, you see . . .' She paused. Then her voice took on a note of—what was it? Excitement? Tension? Glee? No, I realised; this was triumph.

She said, '447 Addison Road, this house and

these gardens and those outbuildings, the jade, the lacquer cabinet, it all belongs, you see, to—me.'

CHAPTER FOUR

In the first place, Cranford is in possession of the Amazons; all the holders of houses, above a certain rent, are women.

Mrs Gaskell began her book with those words in 1853. I first read them one hundred and nine years later, and even then it still was absolutely taken for granted that the lack of men was a tragic and a shameful thing. I was twelve and attitudes were only just slowly beginning to change from what they had been in the earlier part of Queen Victoria's reign. Women were still supposed to live by for, through and with men. Without them women seemed diminished in other people's eyes, and felt worthless themselves too. In actual fact they really were worth much less, financially, socially, professionally and in every other measurable way.

Cranford used to be a set book for girls receiving a restricted, ladylike education. The book's opening lines stayed stuck in my memory because when I first read them, as a holiday task, I felt a thump of recognition, suddenly realising that Portheglos where I spent every summer was in possession of the Amazons too, and so was Woodleigh, the old-fashioned school for dim girls where my mother got a job with a free place for me thrown in, and so was my whole life. In those days it felt as though I never, absolutely never met any men.

And now I'm back to square one. In possession of the Amazons.

*   *   *

My husband left me, I was made redundant, I was diagnosed with breast cancer.

It was a bad year, not helped by the nest emptying, as our son Luke went to college. But that's enough of the doom and gloom, because things cheered up after that. It turned out that the biopsy result was 'a false positive', as they called it. It said 'malignant carcinoma' on the form, which, being long-sighted, I could read from the far side of the doctor's desk, but once removed, the lump was analysed again and proved to be benign after all. So that was all right. And there's always work available for a good lexicographer so I set up as an independent consultant and even had offers from my former employers, at a rather better rate than they were paying me when I was on their staff. Being free and freelance, I would soon have saved enough to take myself on my own version of dream holidays. Stuart and I

33

never even went to a Spanish beach or on a package to Florida, though I suspect either might have been cheaper than our annual cottage in Wales. But Stuart got hives in the sun, I got bored on beaches, Luke wanted to sail, surf and fish. There was always some reason for not going anywhere more exciting, perhaps—to be honest—a residual snobbery that made us cut off our noses to spite our faces; if we couldn't afford the kind of travelling preferred by 'people like us' then we wouldn't travel at all.

But I had a long-standing dream. I longed to go stargazing in the desert, where you can see the wonders of the heavens blazing out of clear, dark skies. Arizona is speckled with the glass of giant telescopes, all set out ready for people like me; they call us astronomical tourists. Or I could go to Israel, to a hotel in the Negev, unpolluted by lighting, where there is a special telescope for watching the sun. I would gaze at the fiery, flamelike prominences on its surface. And one day I was determined to make it down under, visit my mother and see the Southern Cross.

Stuart could never get the point of it, and in the last period of our marriage, after he'd started hating me, said it was exactly the kind of abstract, nitpicking hobby I would go for. 'You don't really care about people or feelings, you're so bloody prissy—honestly, Vick, you can't go through life concentrating on

34

irrelevant things like linguistics and astronomy. I wish you weren't so . . .'

'Inhuman? Impersonal? Detached? Dispassionate? Remote?' I offered.

'There you go again, a bloody walking thesaurus.'

'I like exact language,' I said, and he replied:

'What does it matter what I call it? You know what I mean.'

'How can I know what you mean if you don't say the right words?' And Luke intoned:

'Boring. Change the record. You two are always bickering.'

Physical separation was only the recognition of an emotional fact. Stuart had found, not another woman but an ideal I couldn't share. No, even worse, for he might have acquired some enthusiasm that left me as cold as my stargazing left him—golf, say, or stamp collecting—and I'd have been thrilled (no: relieved; or do I mean encouraged?) that he'd found a hobby to occupy him without me. But my sensible, down-to-earth, materialistic husband, working at the time as bursar of an Oxford college, *got religion.* This man, in whose conversation God had only featured as an expletive, was transformed before my eyes. He started going to church and prayer meetings.

I, on the other hand, was born without what some famous atheist once called 'a God-shaped space in my consciousness'. My upbringing left me marked by other lessons, for example my school (being my home too) gave me an ineradicable work ethic, an overdeveloped sense of duty and the tendency to defer gratification. But years of daily chapel-going never did anything but bore me.

I could just about manage to keep out of it all and ignore Stuart's new passion so long as it remained private. But then he became a deacon and soon afterwards decided his God was calling him into the priesthood. So divorced from reality had he become that he expected to have his own parish with me—of all people—in it as the vicar's helpmeet.

We tried to compromise for a while. He kept up a public pretence that I was too busy to go to church and tried to be tolerant when Luke steered clear, saying in a wounded, disappointed tone, 'Give him time.'

I just didn't listen when Stuart talked pious and averted my eyes from his bent head while he said a silent grace at my secular table. What I really couldn't take was the pause before he rolled over on to me in bed, a moment in which, I suddenly realised, he was asking some kind of blessing on love-making, screwing, the matrimonial sacrament—whatever he called it didn't matter for that silent prayer managed to ruin it for me, such as *it* ever was.

So when Stuart was offered a curacy up in the Wirral, I refused to go. We sold the house in North Oxford and with my half of the proceeds I bought a flat. My cousin Gayle heard I was househunting and rang to tell me exactly what I was to do. She said a friend of hers was getting married to a woman called Nina Gillespie—

'You mean the television reporter?' I interrupted.

'Yes, but that's beside the point, do pay attention, Vicky. Nina's selling her flat, it's not been advertised yet, so you ring her quickly, now, I'll give you the number. . .' Her decisive voice provoked the desire to disobey. But it was good advice with the London property market being notoriously nightmarish at the time. Nina Gillespie was pleased to do a private deal, and remarkably painlessly and fast I found myself settled in a two-bedroomed conversion in Hampstead with a tree-top rustling against the sitting-room window and an ingenious kitchen slotted into what must once have been a linen cupboard.

Nina Gillespie had lived starkly. Even when she showed me round before moving out, the place looked very bare, white paint and black leather chairs with nothing lying around. I like things tidy too, but also cosy. On Nina's stripped floorboards I laid a subtly faded Persian carpet; I bought some cheap greystained wooden furniture from Ikea and a few abstract prints—not that I had a clue what they were about but I liked the shapes and colours. No more hand-coloured engravings of the Oxford colleges for me. Stuart and I had never been able to afford nice things or exciting holidays, because he had to support his widowed mother in residential care. But he was surprised when I didn't fight over the stuff in our Oxford house, and put on a wounded expression when I told him I was starting a life that would not only be new but also different.

I have to admit that those first months of being alone were among the best of my life— with one reservation—and I'm still happy there three years later in spite of the family from hell who have moved to live on the other side of the party wall in the house next door. I manage to avoid antagonising them by never reacting to jeers or meeting their eyes when I see the yobbo kids in the street, maintaining a non-confrontational, uncritical demeanour even when they scatter their rubbish around our front garden or play music full-volume in the small hours. I don't sleep much anyway, being what a despairing doctor once called terminally insomniac. The thump-thump-screech through the wall seems oddly less isolating than Stuart's even, oblivious breaths. And I can always put on my headphones and drown out other noises with the World Service, God's gift to the sleepless. By day I play my own discs, assertive piano and organ music by Bach.

'But you never have any fun,' Gayle accuses,

echoing Stuart who used to complain that I was a stranger to fun and said I even invested star-gazing with some cosmic significance beyond pure pleasure. My idea of fun isn't theirs. I hate big parties, drunk people and competitive conversation, showing-off (by me or anyone else) just embarrasses me, I don't like glitz. Yes, Gayle, I have fun, but it's my own variety. I whizz round London on my bike, I swim lengths, fast, neatly, taking pleasure in my own competence, I make discoveries about language, I marvel at other people's discoveries about the stars. For the last two years I've done what I like.

But it was always going to be easier to escape from a dead marriage than from the terrifyingly vital clutches of my own extended family.

It was my own fault. I shouldn't ever have started visiting Aunt Elena in the first place.

But then, I was sorry for her, and I owed her, it was for old times' sake, and she'd been so very pressing at Uncle Bertram's funeral, swallowing me up in her huge, soft, smothering stranglehold of lusciously soft fur—I couldn't think why she was wearing it, in a stifling late June—and black lace draperies, and the smells of Guerlain's Mitsouko, eucalyptus from her suede gloves, peppermint she'd sucked in the car, the Turkish tobacco she still occasionally smoked. It all drowned the hot oil fumes—fuel and frying—that hovered in the motionless air.

39

'Little Victoria, it's dear little Vicky, but so pale and wan—this won't do.' Pulling back, she put her finger under my chin, lifting my face to gaze into it with her commanding, kohl-rimmed black eyes. 'Now you are in London again you shall come to visit me, we shall talk, yes?'

We were moving towards the chapel in one of the lawyers' Inns, where the atheist Bertram's funeral service was to take place. It was one of those boiling hot days when London streets are full of unappealingly bare-topped men. One could only admire the stamina of those who made themselves wear suits—or worse, today, academic or clerical robes.

As several gaudily clad clerical dignitaries swooped towards Elena, I edged out of the limelight into a back pew, beside a sniffing stranger and behind some broad-shouldered men who completely blocked my view, which was fine by me.

There was a time when I enjoyed the theatre of a decent wedding or funeral, and I still admire the words of the old-fashioned prayer book just as poetry even though I've never been able to summon up the slightest belief in any of the doctrine. After living through Stuart's getting religion, I didn't even like being a non-participating member of the audience.

Very soon after moving into the new flat I'd

become friendly with my downstairs neighbour, a retired psychiatrist called Fidelis Berlin, who had recently started taking Hebrew lessons and instruction about Judaism from an Orthodox acquaintance. She'd arrived in a children's transport from Germany in 1939 and was brought up by Welsh Methodists. Fidelis told me that she'd never taken any interest in her Jewish roots before and I told her that although my unknown American father had been Jewish I never had either, so she invited me to come down and join in. At the time I'm describing, the summer of Uncle Bertram's death, I'd only sat in on a couple of lessons but it was enough to make me feel justified in standing in a stony silence during the hymns and during the prayers sitting up as though I was balancing a book on my head.

Then the orator (a former cabinet minister) began to read a depressingly impersonal eulogy in one of those soggy monotones that should be prescribed instead of sleeping pills. I often doze in lectures or sermons. It's in bed at night that I can't sleep.

On this occasion I did try to listen, because although I'd grown up with the dogma that Bertram was a great man and had even lived in his house for much of one year, I really didn't know much else about him. He was a distant figure, tall and cadaverously thin, especially in contrast to his buxom wife. He had straps of thin hair pasted to his high domed skull and a

41

bristly moustache, slightly narrower than his lips, its grey hairs edged with a rusty colour due, I now realise, to pipe tobacco. As a child I thought it was tomato soup. Uncle Bertram never joined in at any family events, never came on holiday to Portheglos, and when visiting his house, I knew we had to whisper outside his closed study door, an intimidating room, dark-walled, book-filled, smoke-impregnated, where all the pictures were framed sepia photographs of mountain peaks. At meals around his dining-table we females chatted though he hardly spoke, for (I'd been told) he was always pondering and analysing. While we were still eating, he'd push his chair back and stalk speechless from the room to go and make more important discoveries. In the early sixties he was awarded the Nobel prize for some incomprehensible revelation to do with the nature of bacteria.

The speaker could have been reading the *Who's Who* entry aloud. Born in 1903, school at Rugby, studied both medicine and biology at Trinity College, Cambridge, won a starred first and a fellowship at his college, did research in bacteriology, at home and abroad, visiting Australia (Melbourne University) and Tokyo before taking up a post at Addenbrooke's, then some useful years in the United States and work 'out East', before coming back home to do some kind of secret boffinry during the war, which was followed by research posts and visiting fellowships, batting to and fro between America and England on classified jobs for the two governments.

One of the broad-shouldered men whispered to another, 'Porton', and the other whispered back, 'And Nancekuke.' Then one of them glanced round. I didn't meet his glance but I knew the names. Porton Down is the secret government research station in Dorset where they deal in germ warfare; study it, prepare to defend us against it, or even, for all an ordinary citizen knows, prepare to wage it. Nancekuke, officially an air force establishment down the coast from Portheglos, was actually its Cornish outpost, not very far from Portheglos and a cause of local anxiety. Nobody would ever say what was manufactured there.

'Bertram Kittermaster had done the state some service', the orator gnomically said, explaining the knighthood and the other public honours. Then Bertram went back to academia, and a series of ever more distinguished public posts. The Nobel prize really marked the moment when he'd come to the end of doing research. After that, we heard, he'd exerted an increasing influence behind the scenes as a scientific adviser to governments of both colours.

I suddenly had a flash of memory: my mother at the kitchen table in the matron's flat at Woodleigh, reading aloud a snide para in

43

Private Eye, about Uncle Bertram. The famous Mr Knowall. Or was it, by then, Sir Fixit? He'd given advice on a subject not his own which was followed and turned out to be wrong. My mother had sounded pleased, I thought, but when I asked her why she denied it and said she was really angry, how dare anyone criticise the great man? Except his relations, I suppose she meant, though they hardly did; just a raised eyebrow or a knowing smile about his idiosyncrasies and selfishness. Bertram help with the washing up, do the cooking, change a light bulb, sweep the drive, sit on the beach with the girls? What an idea.

Drone, drone . . . the committee for this, the working group for that, the council for the other. The establishment incarnate.

Even in this shady church it was boiling hot. Light seeped through coloured windows.

Regular contributor to serious radio and television programmes: *The Brains Trust, Question Time.* A power and an influence in the land.

A baby was wailing somewhere further forward. I fanned myself with the service sheet. A thin, grey-haired man across the aisle smiled sympathetically. Within a nano-second my imagination had sprinted through a complete romantic scenario: we leave together, get talking, get together—and the rest. As usual. I hadn't given up hope yet. I'm not proud of it, but I promised to tell you the whole story and what I'm like is part of it.

Eminence grise to Prime Ministers, confidant at the Palace . . .

My third cousin Patience came down the aisle with a crying infant, smiling ruefully right and left, mouthing, 'Sorry, sorry.' I didn't know she'd had another. How out of touch I'd become, without my mother around to keep up with the family gossip.

President of a whole list of societies, chairman of a couple of Royal Commissions, Honorary Fellow of this university, Honorary Doctor of that one, Honorary Bencher of this Inn of Court . . .

That baby might be Patience's grandchild, I thought with a slight thrill of dismay. She and I were the same age. Were we really old enough for that? Actually, yes. It seemed a depressing thought, far more depressing than this supposedly mournful ceremony.

The speaker had reached the home straight with a speedy rundown of Bertram's personal life. Elena, the Hungarian émigrée, beautiful, accomplished and aristocratic, who had become so gracious a wife, mother and hostess. Their two daughters. Twin grandchildren. Love for the high mountains, a good climber in his day. Sympathy, pride and, at last, the next hymn. Then we were released.

I followed the crowd into the Great Hall, a room full of cousins, the Kittermaster connection having turned out in force, on this

45

occasion even including the men. They enjoyed a funeral, especially one whose baked meats (or, in this case, sour sherry) were shared by what looked like the whole British 'establishment'. A chorus of gruff voices was praising 'a jolly good send-off'.

It was so long since I'd attended a family gathering that I didn't recognise those I should know, and wasn't even sure which ones were relations. There were a few I remembered and others who had frequently-publicised faces, like the Booker prize-winning author Paddy Kittermaster, the Shakespearean actor Chris Heneage and the Junior Minister of Health Joanna Chambers. The clan didn't get together so often any more, or if they did I hadn't been included much, in the dozen years since my mother went off to manage a holiday village in Fiji. In fact one of the great uncles expressed surprise to see me. 'Thought you were in Tahiti. Gauguin. No, New Guinea. Cannibals. Or was it Samoa?'

'Football?' I offered.

'I could have sworn they said down under somewhere.' He seemed obscurely indignant to see me in England so I apologised and said I had to go and talk to an aunt.

I'm not very good at parties, and in self-defense have learnt to cope with them by moving purposefully and smiling past all the indifferent strangers to some imaginary friend on the far side of the room. Moving thus, I caught titbits of conversation. How well you look, how ill he looks, didn't see old Billy, d'you see young Willy—the social language I've never quite mastered. I heard comments about the choir—'too shrill'—and the politician's eulogy, which had been thought a bit dry.

'Left out quite a few facts,' said one elderly man, to which his even older companion replied:

'And people.'

'Hah!' All he needed was a walrus moustache to blow through; this old chap was like a cartoon clubman.

'Bloody good thing, if you ask me,' his companion said.

'How right you are, we don't want anyone stirring the shit now.'

'Should be safe enough now old Bertram's gone.'

'D'you know the chap was spotted?'

'You mean he's around somewhere? I'd no idea.'

'It must be some years ago. It was Jack— remember old Jack?—caught sight of him in Hawaii of all places. Or so he claimed.'

'Good God.'

'And then he was spotted in Winnipeg in, '79, and then someone, don't remember who, said they caught sight of him in India, must be a good ten years ago now.'

'Got to keep his head down, what? If he

turned up here—well . . .' The two old men, one pink, smooth, fat and bald, the other gaunt and grey, glanced over their shoulders and together barrelled their way into a corner of the room where they muttered secretively.

'Vicky, hi, all well with you?' My cousin Gayle, as inevitable as a typhoon.

There's a lot to be said for belonging to a large family, or so at least my mother often said as she sent me off into its care the very moment the school term ended. There was always some relation prepared to take me in, whether on holiday down at Portheglos or at their homes, Victorian semi-detached in Hampstead, Edwardian-suburban in Cambridge, Georgian town-centre flats in Edinburgh or a barn conversion in the Cotswolds. I list a few characteristic locations to show the kind of people most Kittermasters are: academic, prosperous, establishment figures who know the ropes and the right people but are never ostentatious.

As a matter of fact, it's a famous name, woven into England's intellectual, religious (Quaker) and social history. Cf. Darwin, Wedgwood, Fry, Huxley. Our family tree is full of successful men who were knighted, one foreign secretary, several social reformers, women pioneers, activists and a painter. It's dotted with heads of colleges, leading medics, one life peer, several knights and a Nobel prize winner, Uncle Bertram himself. In my teens I wanted to use the name, rather than my father's, which was Moss. He'd scarpered (abandoned us? buggered off?) when I was a baby so I didn't remember him. When my mother got the news that he'd died after 'flying' out of a window on a bad acid trip, I, by then in my early teens, thought it all the more unnecessary to make any formal recognition of the fact that six weeks before I was born he and my mother had actually made it to the register office.

But my mother tried to convince me that I was lucky to be spared a burdensome label she'd never managed to live up to. She had hated the fact that 'if you're called Kittermaster teachers always expect you to be clever'. Which she's the first to admit she isn't. I, however, was, but she didn't really care whether I did well in exams, she was just impatient and irritated by my behaviour and appearance. I was small and plain and bad at sports. Recognising me as such, I do wonder now what she thought she was doing every summer, packing me off as a poor relation to the untender mercies of the whole gang. Toughening me up, perhaps.

If so, it didn't work. I was wet and weedy as a child and still am. The difference is that I don't mind any more. I'm perfectly happy as I am, neat and precise, probably very old-fashioned, and much relieved to know that I'll never ever again have to take any notice of games involving bats or balls. A sheltered life as an inhibited introvert suits me fine. I expected to manage perfectly well even if I never did find Mr Right—as long as nobody else ever discovered how much I fantasised about him. Except you. No secrets between us.

Gayle greeted me with the old familiar breezy patronage. Gayle's an example of why it isn't necessarily wonderful to be part of a large extended family, unless you are one of the successful ones. You can't help knowing that whatever you achieve seems worthless in comparison with other relatives who have invariably, inevitably done much more, much better.

Gayle always treats me like a poor *thing*—one with no gumption, no get up and go. One of nature's suckers.

She said, 'You want to be careful, Vicky, I know you, always a soft touch, I can just see you getting sucked into Elena's clutches, you'll be running her errands in no time. Steer clear, I should.'

Of course she would, Gayle had known about looking after number one since the cradle, as well I remembered from having often taken the rap for her naughtiness during those dread holidays with her family. And it was almost worse when nobody found out what we were doing in time to stop us. Those dares and tests, those adventures into tidal caves or down crumbling cliffs, the stuff of

50

children's books, might be thrilling on the page but in real life were all my idea of hell. I couldn't run along a wall without falling off, I couldn't surf the big breakers, I couldn't stay on a horse. I wanted to be left alone, allowed to be 'that funny little thing, curled up in a corner with her book'.

'D'you know all these people, Gayle?' I asked.

' 'Course not, nor did Bertram. I shouldn't think most of this lot had seen him for years. If ever—he wasn't exactly matey. But you know how Englishmen always turn out for funerals.'

I smiled, and she went on, 'My writer will have to talk to them.'

'Your writer, Gayle?'

'We're planning to commission a family history.'

'Are you? D'you think it's a commercial subject?'

'If you mean, do I think it will be a best seller, I'd say it's not impossible, but it's to be written first and then we'll see if a publisher's interested, and if not, I'll have it printed privately. There must be masses of material, I can't think why nobody's done it already. Actually I've suddenly thought—Vicky, what about you? You've always been bookish and you've got the time, would you like to do it?'

I refrained from telling her I'd rather clean the floor with my tongue, and said instead, 'I don't think I have quite the same feelings about the family as you do, Gayle, thanks all the same, but I'm sure there won't be any problem finding someone who'd be glad of the subject for a thesis.'

'Pity. Are you sure? I'll pay a good whack.'

'Victoria, my dear, and how are you now? How's the . . . ?' My great aunt Connie made a waving gesture at my bosom.

'I'm absolutely fine, thank you,' I said curtly.

'I was so sorry to hear about it, have you had to have horrid sick-making treatment, poor one? I remember when my friend Irma, you won't remember her but she had a growth on—'

'Vicky's perfectly all right, Aunt,' Gayle shouted into the old ear, gripping Connie's arm and firmly directing her into a group of her own contemporaries. I had always envied and been frightened of Gayle's decisiveness.

Gayle had become another of the famous Kittermasters, the founder, owner and managing director of one of the fastest growing companies in Europe. Its business was making miniatures: all those things travellers need to pack in sizes small enough not to weigh down the baggage: tiny little books printed on India paper, quarter-size brushes (hair, tooth, clothes), weeny little tubes of toothpaste and cans of talcum powder, dolly-sized jars of cosmetics.

Glossy magazines were always running pieces about Gayle's lavish home and happy marriage and clever children and witty taste in clothes, black today, of course, but both coat and turban-shaped hat made of silky-soft suede with a pattern of little holes punched in it. Since Stuart and I split up Gayle had occasionally invited me to dinner. Her idea of the kind of man I'd suit was instructive. They were all old, or seemed so, and always had something wrong with them, a land agent with a stammer so bad that one literally could not converse with him, a banker who'd been disfigured in a car crash or a singer with raging psoriasis. I have my dreams, far too many dreams, but these men didn't fit any of them. Gayle turned back to me and I said:

'It's like the Black Hole of Calcutta in here.'

'Hot flushes?' Gayle asked.

'Certainly not, d'you mind?'

'Could be, you must be—what, fifty?'

'Forty-six.'

'Are you on HRT?'

'No, Gayle, I'm not on HRT, I don't need it.'

'You could be wrong, I'll give you my gynae's address, I'd say it's time for taking more care of yourself, Vicky, what about a health farm, I know of a very good one that won't be too expensive for you, and I'll put you on to my hairdresser, you could do with lowlights, say you're my cousin, she can do wonders . . .'

Elena was moving past us, seeming

53

somehow isolated from her husband's colleagues, admirers and relations. She planted the flat of her hands on her breastbone, cast her gaze upwards—one of bereavement's classic poses.

'My life is over,' she announced.

Katie, hurrying to Elena's side, protested. 'Mother, no!'

'Actually she'll enjoy her freedom, the old man always treated her like a slave,' Gayle murmured in my ear.

'He was everything to me, everything, without him I am nothing.'

'A touch of the drama queens,' Gayle said, and when I asked if that wasn't a bit unfeeling she went on, 'Not unfeeling at all, I really sympathise, she's going to miss the status. No more invitations to Downing Street or Buckingham Palace.'

Katie and Christina led their mother away, one with her arm round the bowed shoulders, the other arm in arm.

I followed them out, waiting as the three black-clad women—Elena and Katie even wore ostentatiously thick black stockings and mantillas—were helped into a black car. Fat raindrops were beginning to fall on the dusty grass in the central courtyard. I saw the grey-haired man, who had not glanced at me again, unfurl a sleek umbrella and walk away. As I stepped outside torrents suddenly rushed from the sky.

I should have told Gayle I could manage my own life. I should have mentioned my new commission, a good two years of really well-paid thesaurus work for a software company. I should have boasted about Luke's essay prize. I should have said that the advantage of cutting my own, still naturally dark hair into short wispy curls instead of going to her fancy hairdresser was that it didn't matter getting it crushed under my swimming cap or bike helmet; that I actually liked being out in the rain.

I felt as though the water was showering me clean and free of family piety. It had not been a jolly good send-off, I thought. It had been hypocritical to use the formal service for a card-carrying atheist, and nobody, except his widow, had spoken about the old man as though they really cared that he was dead.

And—though I didn't notice it then or in the twenty months after that day—nobody had mentioned the name of a man called Justin Lang.

CHAPTER FIVE

Beijing was the Forbidden City and the Summer Palace and the Great Wall of China and a Chrysanthemum Festival, a glut of art and culture to satisfy all the punters. A local guide escorted the party round because union rules forbade foreigners to lecture at these tourist honey-pots.

Mr Feuerstein had a sick turn when they were at the Tombs of the Nobles and whole series of effortful problems flashed through Hilly's mind, beginning with the notorious frightfulness of this country's hospitals, but mercifully he recovered quickly and travelled on with the group to Kaifeng, looking all the time more frail and more like a pilgrim on his last, pious journey.

Kaifeng proved to have no attractions except for its name in Jewish history. Ari told Hilly he'd known what to expect and she said:

'Well, of course, you've been here before, you must have known.' Upon which, he admitted, as he hadn't before, that he'd never been to China in his life and had been lecturing entirely from second-hand knowledge. He'd researched, looked at photos, read books, done a lot of homework.

'But this is your subject!' she cried.

'Yeah, but I could never swing a grant to get me here.'

It wasn't the first time Hilly had found herself abroad with a specialist lecturer who was less experienced than he or she had told the travel company and she usually reported the fact when she got home. It was a common scam to rip off a free trip, whereby the cheating, self-styled expert conned company

56

and customers alike. But in this case she wouldn't complain that Ari was letting the brand-name down since, as he said, he'd done his homework so well as to seem entirely plausible. Maybe his information, authoritatively delivered as he showed the pax round, was really inaccurate, but if so nobody else noticed or knew better and she couldn't see that it mattered much.

In any case, in Kaifeng at least, everything relevant had long since vanished. The site of its disappeared synagogue or the fragments of Hebrew in the municipal museum required to be seen with the eye of faith, as Ari lectured to a credulous but disappointed audience about the Jews' long history in this part of China— having come via the Silk Road in the eighth century, their presence confirmed by Marco Polo, an assimilated yet distinct part of the community.

Mrs Harpner had become more and more disgruntled as the days passed. It was too hot, too windy, the dust gave her sinus. The acrid, pervasive smell, to old China hands the country's specific, characteristic identifier, caused her to go round with a scent-doused handkerchief pressed over her nose. She complained of the incessant noise—traffic, trams screeching, the high, shrill chatter of the native Chinese. She objected to the endless queues and was disgusted by the way people hawked and spat, she was frightened of going off the tourist track because when they did, squads of interested, giggling locals gathered to stare at the foreigners. She'd never understood why Chuck cared so much about Sino-Judaic history in the first place. As for the food—well, enough said, though of course she went on saying it.

Every group had one grumbler, Hilly knew it was one of the inescapable rules. She uttered some automatic soothing, and Ari said, 'Never mind, Mrs H, you'll like Shanghai, it's the Paris of the East.'

Certainly it provided unlimited shopping opportunities, though it was no longer the sophisticated metropolis of the years before the war and Communism. But Shanghai turned out to be nothing if not consumer orientated, even if many of the consumers envisaged were looking for goods and services of which Mrs Harpner knew only from the pages of tabloid newspapers and crime fiction.

This town had been full of non-Chinese communities until the Cultural Revolution, and Jews, Ari said, had flourished here, for Shanghai had been a focus of Jewish immigration to China from the middle of the nineteenth century Russians escaping pogroms via Siberia and Harbin, Sephardis from Baghdad and Bombay, Germans in the 1930s. He handed out copies of a list of places for the enthusiasts to visit. The ghetto, though, as he warned, 'There's not really anything much left to see of that,' three Jewish schools, four cemeteries and seven synagogues, one of them now creepily occupied by the mental hospital's isolation ward and another forming part of the Friendship Store.

Mrs Harpner's shopping went badly in the Friendship Store. She wondered if it was a judgement on her for co-operating in the desecration of a holy place, for there were no embroidered silk robes she liked in a large enough size or cashmere shawls in a colour she'd wear. As for the dinner services—well, she could find better for half the price back home. But the other women came away with sackfuls of fabrics and souvenirs. That evening the Peace Hotel, which had formerly been the Sassoon Building, belonging to wealthy Jewish settlers, laid on 'a banquet'. As Hilly had warned when the journey began, every formal dinner was called a banquet. At their first, in Harbin, Mrs Harpner had left the table at a run on finding half of a tiny skull in her stew. Another, less susceptible lady had remarked with detached objectivity that it looked as though cooked duck or chicken meant literally that—the whole carcass, roughly chopped, was apparently chucked into the pot with the other ingredients. At the banquet in Kaifeng Mrs Harpner had stood at her place holding her chopsticks motionless in the soup pan as it bubbled on its little portable burner on the dining-table.

'What do you think you're doing now?' her husband asked in a long-suffering tone.

'Disinfecting these chopsticks at boiling point,' she replied with self-righteous dignity. 'I told you about bacteria surviving in bamboo chopsticks, it said so in the *American Inquirer.*'

The Peace Hotel in Shanghai was another matter, a mansion of the 1920s still with wood-panelled rooms and some of the original bathrooms installed for Victor Sassoon, a Jew from Baghdad who ploughed the fortune he had made out of the opium trade into property in Shanghai, and into horses. Ari quoted his favourite saying: 'There is only one race greater than the Jews, and that is the Derby.'

Hilly was thinking that Ari had lifted that straight from the Lonely Planet guide to China when Mrs Harpner burst out:

'Monstrous! How dare you? Did you hear what he said?'

'Sorry, what's the problem?' Ari asked.

'You rude boy, what do you understand, so know-it-all, rude ignorant boy in those ragged clothes—a disgrace—and what, I'd like to know,' she concluded, 'what's it to you? You're certainly not in China for our sakes, that's only too obvious, and considering what we've spent on—'

'Now, Mother, that's—' her husband began.

Ari, his attention sharply aroused, perhaps, Hilly thought, for the first time this trip, turned an unexpectedly boyish and rueful charm on to the older woman. 'I know,' he murmured, 'you've had it up to here with me, right? I've been thinking about our history too much and not paid enough mind to—'

'No, no, not at all,' those within conversation range murmured soothingly. 'She didn't mean it.'

'Mrs Harpner did mean it and she was quite right,' he said. 'I've been distracted. The weight of the past lies on us, the vibes from all those others who were here before us, our people in an alien land, it kind of blows my mind.'

Hilly thought he both meant what he said and realised it would be effective. He went on, to a listening room, 'Take my family, just another ordinary Jewish story of hell on earth, everyone's got them back home. My grandmother managed to reach Shanghai from Manchuria, she was alone with her little boy, but this is where it gets unreal, she met a Brit, and he saved her, got her out of here with her son.'

Nods, head-shakes, sympathetic noises went round the room. Mr Feuerstein said, 'God had a purpose for her life.'

'Well, in that case, God knows what,' Ari said flippantly. 'Actually she died when my dad was a kid, he hardly knew her himself as far as I know, not that I do know much.'

Mr Feuerstein's hawkish profile was projected in shadow on to the wall beside him.

61

Straggling hair, uncut since he left home, and an expression, Hilly suddenly thought, that should be described as exalted, made him resemble her idea of a prophet, someone fierce and righteous out of the Old Testament, as his voice cracked and quavered and his pointed fingers trembled.

'You should know this,' he told Ari. He said something in Hebrew, and then, perhaps for the benefit of Hilly, the only non-Jew there, said in English, 'Honour thy father and thy mother that thy days may be long on this earth.'

Ari said, 'My dad scarpered out of the kibbutz leaving my mother behind.'

'But he was still alive, still your father.'

'I never saw anything of him, he was—well, he had a secret job.'

'Mossad?' one of the Englishmen asked knowledgeably. 'Secret service?'

'That is not a subject to discuss, but no matter what he did, the father survived. So many of our people lost their families, their history was stolen from them, and you willingly abandon yours?' Mr Feuerstein accused. 'And you call yourself a historian?'

CHAPTER SIX

Not long after Bertram's funeral I was summoned to tea in Addison Road. Katie was living there, but hadn't come home from work yet, so Elena and I sat together in the garden. The lawn had been rough-cut but the flower beds were untended although the ancient wistaria still flowered on the back wall of the house, a shaggy syringa smelt delicious and unpruned roses still produced some tenacious blooms.

I arrived sweating having biked from the newly opened British Library, too warmly dressed in a grey jersey suit. Elena opened the door as I was simultaneously pulling off the helmet and wiping sweat from my brow with the back of my arm.

'My dear, you still ride a bicycle in London? It's not safe,' she cried.

'I'm very careful,' I assured her.

'And the steep hills!'

'Don't worry, Aunt Elena, this bike's got a dozen gears.'

'From here to Hampstead, it's impossible. I shall send you home in a taxi.'

Elena was in lace-trimmed flowered voile, her hair piled on top of her head, Edwardian style. Her own grandmother might have looked much the same in the old days of the Austro-Hungarian empire. We sat on upright chairs at a round table with an embroidered cloth and laid with the kind of afternoon tea I didn't think anyone had any more, triangular cucumber sandwiches with white bread and rolls of asparagus in brown, iced sponge, slices of heavy fruit loaf, thickly buttered, with lidded pots of jam and honey round which wasps hovered. Elena rinsed the porcelain cups out with hot water from a spirit burner, before filling them with straw-coloured liquid from a tarnished silver pot. Yes, I remembered, even at Portheglos she never did lower herself to providing thick ginger-coloured tea in a gritty pottery mug.

I'd lodged here during the gap between school and university but didn't remember much about the house then; I think I was so busy enjoying my first freedom (in the gaps of learning shorthand and typing) that bed and breakfast at Addison Road didn't register.

Now, at an age and stage to notice such things, I saw that the house was in a bad state of repair, long overdue for redecoration. In the downstairs loo there was a bucket and a handwritten note explaining that because the plug was broken, one had to fill the bucket with water from the basin and pour it down. A plastic bollard, presumably stolen from some road-works, stood as a warning where the passage carpet had a trip-you-up hole in it and the wallpaper was peeling off in the hall. Bertram's study was not merely untouched since his death, it had never been redecorated or altered since the 1950s. I wasn't trendy enough to realise in mid-1997 how soon the jagged, jazzy, strident curtain fabric, which screamed 'Festival of Britain', would come round into high fashion again, as would the awkward wooden rhombus that had been designed as a coffee table—covered, still, with academic journals—and the moulded plastic chairs with black metal legs, and the Bakelite, asymmetrical bowl in which decades' worth of paperclips were rusting away.

Nonetheless Elena's behaviour implied the necessity of keeping up the relevant standards of the great house in Hungary her ancestors lived in, though she can't have remembered much of it having been only ten when war broke out. But in her imagination proper standards required not only a proper afternoon tea, but also properly deferential middle-aged daughters remaining at home and subservient to their mothers, as, when Katie came in, I saw that she still, or again, was. Christina had got away and stayed away, so far. At this time she was in America with a new partner and small twin sons.

Elena behaved maternally towards me. I wondered whether I'd forgotten some closer relationship between her and me as a child. Had I confided in her during the long cold summers at Portheglos? My memories of them were patchy.

It's supposed to be a truism that the summers of one's childhood were always beautiful, but if you ask me to describe mine I'd visualise cowering in the inadequate shelter of a striped canvas windbreak and trying to get out of my wet swimsuit without being seen by the others or leaving sand in my knickers. In that exposed cove, lashed by north-west winds and thunderous breakers, groups from each cottage set up camp for the day.

I suppose Elena must have been on the beach too, though she never looked the type for stoical English picnics. I tried to remember whether she'd been sitting with the Mummies, at the ready with towels and first aid. Or had I stayed behind with her in the house and *confided* into that generous maternal bosom? I was clearly expected to do so now and pour out the full saga of Stuart and why I left him, my operation and how it left me, my life and loves. It was a relief when Katie joined us.

She came down the steps into the garden, a dramatic figure wearing a large crystal on an amulet, on very high heels, with her pitch black hair and white face and lips a slash as crimson as her flowing dress. She'd been, she said, at a reading.

'Poetry?' I asked.

'My dear.' She gave a treble laugh on a descending scale. 'It's my day for the Princess, I was held up trying to calm her. The stars are not in her favour. Now you, Vicky, when were you born, was it in March?'

'September.'

'Ah, of course, I see it now, Virgo, careful, conscientious, orderly. Show me your hand.'

'D'you read palms too?

'Katarina has decided she is a sensitive,' Elena said.

'A psychic, it's the Romany blood,' Katie said boastfully.

'Romany—such nonsense—and in Bertram's child!'

'Gosh, Katie, astrology and palmistry,' I said. 'Whatever did Uncle Bertram say?'

'Oh, Father. He never had any *vision*.'

'Your father was the most brilliant scientist of his generation,' Elena corrected her.

'He was an earthbound mortal through and through, I'm afraid,' Katie said.

'We could not be doing with all this nonsense, he and I,' Elena announced.

'Mama was brainwashed so she has no patience with me, or with Chrissie either.'

'What's she doing these days?' I asked.

'Chrissie may be all sympathy, but she's very material, she can't see past the barriers,' Katie said.

'Take no notice of Katie's nonsense, Christina's a nurse. Now, Vicky, tell us about you,' Elena commanded, but Katie carried on:

'What Mother means is that Chrissie holds the hands of the dying, up to the very portal of their new lives, but she's too down-to-earth to see beyond them as I do. There's too much Kittermaster in her for true insight, like you, Vicky, you're always so sensible.' Katie didn't mean it as a compliment. But common sense is a useful quality and so Elena was to find it in the next months.

I became a regular visitor, partly because she wanted me to come but more, I realised, because I found I was happier with some kind of family obligation. It gave a pattern to my life if I felt obliged to slog out to Kensington at least once a week. Elena took to living in a kind of time warp, as though the celebrity of the famous man's home and the public recognition she'd shared had survived his death. In retrospect I can see she was already failing before her final illness was diagnosed. When she mentioned intrusive reporters and importunate admirers such as those who had regularly pestered Bertram, I think she really believed they'd been bothering her. In fact there were very few visitors or phone calls. Except from me.

I was practical about things nobody who was living in that house could cope with. Though I drew the line at cleaning. Elena took on cleaners and sacked them almost every month. 'Nobody is up to it, only my precious Mrs Beck, oh how I miss that woman, you remember my Mrs Beck?'

She'd have been about a hundred by now, but in fact I did just remember Mrs Beck bustling round the house in a flowered pinny, four foot nothing and gutsy with it, a cockney sparrow who called Elena 'madam' and me 'miss'. I recall my mother, walking to the bus after a visit to Addison Road, telling me how lucky Aunt Elena was to have such a treasure, who cleaned that whole house and did the ironing and washed the windows and prepared the vegetables, all in four hours a day. 'I wonder, Mrs B, do you think you could just mend this sheet—or unpack the shopping—or peel the vegetables?' Elena's requests were phrased as questions, but not questions that expected the answer no.

'Your grandma's a marvel, Marlene, one in a thousand,' Elena said. Marlene (named, like many of her contemporaries, after Dietrich) used to come along with Mrs Beck on Saturdays. She'd sit at the kitchen table with her school books, a resentful big girl with blonde pigtails whose unpleasantly sweaty, salty smell was quite familiar in those days, when the poor didn't use deodorants and virgins were told tampons were only for married women. Mrs Beck had to look after Marlene because her mother had married a no-good Irishman, I'd overheard, before the Mummies said something about little pitchers and long ears and changed the subject. Marlene hated everything: school and home and the Kittermasters. She once told me I was a spoilt brat whose family were all over-privileged snobs and come the revolution they'd hang the lot of us from lamp-posts.

Well, there were no Mrs Becks in Addison Road in the 1990s, nor even their Filipino or Portuguese successors. I once arranged for a firm of spring cleaners but Elena said they had left white marks on a lacquer table, so I gave up on that idea. But I did sometimes get a handyman to come in, and I fixed some things myself. Without me the downstairs lavatory wouldn't ever have been mended or the electrical appliances rewired. I pruned the roses and planted bulbs and even occasionally dealt with Bertram's solicitor.

Tony Paxton of Wootton Hardman was about my age, a burly, brown man, very attractive. Married, of course. He worked at a snail's pace. Admittedly there was no hurry with the formalities. As Bertram's will simply made his wife his executor and left the lot to her, there were no death duties to pay and Elena didn't intend to sell or change anything. It didn't seem worth complaining or chivvying him, and wouldn't have done much good anyway, these things always take ages. I knew a man whose solicitor took more than two years to get probate after his father died.

Elena had got through the 'my life is over' phase within weeks of Bertram's funeral and was soon full of plans. Her holidays used to consist of sitting in some mountain resort's Grand Hotel while Bertram climbed, or in later years walked, to the tops. Now she said she'd go to America and stay with Christina, who was still in San Francisco at the time, or take poor Katie to a Greek island or even go to Hungary. But then she thought the pain

70

might be unbearable. 'I have not been back, since,' she said darkly.

I was in the house with Elena when she had a call from a journalist on the *Argus* and noticed how pleased she looked, at first. She must have been missing the contact with the world of public affairs and publicity. It had been fun for her, living with a celebrity. She'd thrived on calls to ask what Bertram thought about some scientific or political question, requests for quotes or sound bites or predictions, queries about favourite and influential books. She had done that sort of thing for him, she told me many times. 'I chose his music for *Desert Island Discs*, Bartok, Haydn, he was not musical himself, my poor Bertram. And his book of the year, every year. He couldn't have managed these things, he was above them.'

This time, about eight months after he died, the call began with her practised charm. Then I saw her face drain of colour. 'Elena? What is it?' I said. 'Here, shall I deal with this?' I took the telephone and said, 'Victoria Merton here.'

'Lady Kittermaster, please.'

'She isn't feeling very well. Can I help?'

'I'm just checking some facts.'

I asked who was speaking and he gave me his name. I didn't know it, but then he said he was writing a piece about Cambridge in the thirties, all that lot, could I comment on

71

Bertram Kittermaster's connection with his undergraduate contemporaries, the famous Cambridge Spies.

I was what my son Luke would have called gob-smacked, though quickly realised it was the kind of conceivable but implausible connection one might make all these years later. Bertram was the right generation, he could have known Philby and Blunt and all that lot whose names I couldn't even remember. I had never been very interested in those tales of spies, could never even find John le Carré's novels exciting. Of course it had mattered, when I was born in 1950 the fate of the world turned on it, but now the Cold War seemed as remote as the Wars of the Roses. At last I said:

'You've taken me completely by surprise, and as for my aunt, she nearly had a heart attack. What on earth makes you ask that?'

'The name came up.'

'Well, it can jolly well go down. Bertram Kittermaster a spy? I never heard anything so ridiculous.'

'So you won't comment?'

'Won't, can't—there isn't any comment to make. Read his obituaries, ask his colleagues and friends. Anyway, weren't those others all in the Foreign Office? What d'you think he could have spied on? He was a scientist, a doctor, nothing to do with the H-bomb, I promise you.' By this time I was actually laughing. Then, looking across at Elena, who was better but still a bit pale, I went on, 'You'd better be careful what you print.'

He asked more of the same question in different words for a few more minutes, but I guessed he was just flying a kite. Or shaking a tree to see what fell out. Or sucking it to see. He was checking up on everyone famous of that generation, that was all. Still, I had a word with Tony Paxton just in case and he had a word with the editor of the *Argus* at the Garrick one lunchtime and the whole thing died down and was forgotten, except that it was the first moment I realised that Elena herself was ill. Not long afterwards she was told she had lung cancer, chain-smoker Bertram's final legacy. Katie, after months of sniping at her mother, went to pieces. I had to be the one who took Elena to Harley Street for the initial consultation, and to the expensive private clinic for the biopsy and X-ray, and back to the consulting rooms and then back to the clinic. I was there when she first met the surgeon and again when he broke the news that it was cancer and once more when he told her it had spread through the lymph glands and into other organs, including—but she stopped him then. She didn't want to know or think about or even admit it.

'Her generation went in for not admitting things,' Gayle said.

'Maybe it made life more comfortable?' I

73

suggested.

'No, repressed. Think how much easier dealing with medics is for us than poor old Elena, so many men have seen and felt our private bits already.'

Not mine, I thought, but didn't say so. I know I look prim (proper? spinsterish?) but I'd rather other people thought the controlled exterior was just that. There's no need for even my best friends to know it goes all through. I mean, I have been married, I have had another relationship, if an unsuccessful one, but I'm not experienced, in the sense Gayle meant, and I'm not—or, I should say, I wasn't—passionate. Aunt Elena, however, told me no other man than Bertram had ever seen her undressed and she tried to stay modest right up to the end which came mercifully fast and in her own bed. Everything went to the girls in equal shares: the cottage at Portheglos, a little jewellery, some good furniture, money—and the house. Its sale, even allowing for its run-down state and the taxes due, would make both Katie and Christina into millionaires.

CHAPTER SEVEN

After Marguerite Lang's verbal bombshell had exploded in Addison Road, causing the alarm and astonishment she certainly intended, the girls and I were transformed into instant combatants—in my case, however, a deeply reluctant one. Katie having called Christina on her mobile and my message having been left for Mr Paxton, I then occupied the interval before Christina's return in mentally berating myself for ever getting involved. I must have been mad to say I'd be Elena's executor. I should have known it would be nothing but trouble. The estate consisted of a good deal of money, well over seven figures, but the most valuable asset must be the house itself. Without it to sell, the girls' lives weren't going to change, and although I don't think either was unduly grasping they had both made plans based on inheriting that comfortable amount.

When Christina came in hotfoot from a death-bed, the three of us huddled whispering in the hall. 'She says the house wasn't Father's at all, it belonged to her husband,' Katie hissed.

'Don't be silly, that's got to be nonsense, what did Paxton say?'

'He doesn't know, he hasn't checked the title deeds.'

'Why not?' Christina demanded, fixing me in a chilly glare.

'All I know is what he told me.' It had been bad enough having to overcome his secretary's resistance to putting me through to Mr Paxton on his mobile, who was skiing somewhere in

France. I didn't see why I should take the blame for his carelessness.

'But he was Father's executor!'

'One of them, your mother was the other.'

'All the same—'

'He said he hadn't got round to it yet.'

'It's nearly two years!'

'He said it didn't seem urgent since it didn't make any difference to Elena, she was living here anyway and all the money was in a joint account.'

'That must be professional negligence,' Christina complained.

'The law's delays,' Katie quoted.

'So you're telling us Paxton couldn't say whose name's on the title deeds?'

I said, 'I'm sorry, Christina, I'm only passing on what he said, but he's going to get back to us tomorrow.'

'Of course the house was Father's, and he left it to Mother. This woman's totally bonkers, has to be, that money belongs to us, d'you understand?' Christina insisted, leading the way upstairs.

'The money, the money—what does it matter,' Katie wailed, 'compared with love, human feeling . . .'

Marguerite Lang was waiting for us in the boudoir, standing as close as possible to the single-barred electric heater and sipping the time-expired fortified wine Katie had found in a sticky decanter, which might have contained

Madeira or sherry or even vermouth.

The room Elena had called her boudoir was a cubby hole above the rear porch. In it were crammed tables and a desk, a *chaise-longue* and a small rocking chair. The flower-sprigged walls were almost invisible under photos hung frame to frame: Hungarian scenes in sepia, the girls at all ages in black and white and rather a lot of Christina's twins, in Technicolor. It was cold in winter and stuffy in summer, but Elena had been, as her daughters said, 'the boudoir type' and in all that large house, this was the only corner where she had chosen, or been allowed, to impress her personality on her surroundings. The room smelt of Turkish cigarettes and her musky scent, and the imprint of her body still seemed impressed on the numerous cushions. There was nothing of Bertram's in here except for one formal picture showing him in tails and medals beside Elena in feathers and pearls at the Nobel prize ceremony.

Marguerite seemed unperturbed by the silent wait. She was much calmer than me and Katie. Christina was just cross. She said, 'This had better be good,' and with evident satisfaction Marguerite repeated to Christina what she'd already told me and Katie. She owned this house.

Christina used the calm and soothing voice of a professional health care worker which would of course have been properly prudent, if

Marguerite really was mad, but she didn't sound it to me. 'How do you make that out, exactly?'

Marguerite said she was the widow of Justin Lang and had the papers to prove it.

I said I'd never heard of Justin Lang.

'Nor have I,' Katie agreed.

'Don't be silly, Katie, of course you have, but he must have been dead for more than thirty years,' Christina said.

Katie said, 'But I don't know who you mean.'

'Yes you do, he was the boy Father looked after before we were born,' Christina answered.

'Oh—you mean the one we mustn't ever mention, that Justin.'

'Girls, do explain,' I asked.

'Oh Vicky, didn't you ever hear of him? He was this war orphan that Father took on,' Katie said.

'But nobody's mentioned his existence at all.'

'There wasn't any reason to, he wasn't ever part of our lives and I only remembered his name because Mother once said it, and then she told me he wasn't to be spoken of again.'

'But weren't you interested? Curious?' I asked.

'Not really, it was old history, before my time,' Christina said.

'He wasn't talked about at all, I have a

78

feeling he must have done something awful,' Katie said.

'Nonsense, he died young, that's all,' Chrissie said.

Mrs Lang's eyes moved from speaker to speaker with evident pleasure; she was enjoying herself.

'No, wait a minute . . .' Katie pressed the tips of her fingers to her temples. 'It was . . . it must have been one of the cousins, Jake, I think, or maybe Eddie, they were always blurting things out, one of them was here for lunch and said the name, Justin, and Mother told him to be quiet and Father got up and left the table. Might he have been a dropout or a junkie, d'you suppose?'

'More likely it was too painful to mention,' Christina said. 'It's very common, you know, to draw a veil over the thought of a lost child.'

'You know Father would never have talked about anything personal anyway' Katie said.

'What about Elena?' I asked.

'She didn't meet Father till she got here in 1956, did she, Chrissie. I don't know how old Justin would have been—'

'Twenty-six,' Mrs Lang interrupted.

'Well, we were born in '57 and '58, and Justin must have died when we were tinies, no wonder we forgot him,' Katie said.

'What does it matter anyway?' Christina said. 'Whoever he was, whatever happened to him, it can't have anything to do with our

79

family home. Father moved here before the war, what are you saying, that he left it to this Justin? Since he died decades before Father did—'

Smiling, using a level, gentle voice, Marguerite corrected her. 'Justin died in 1986—and this house was his property.' She was openly gleeful, for some reason enjoying her task of delivering what would be bad news, if it was true.

'I'm afraid you're talking nonsense, Mrs Lang', Christina said in her most unemotional tone. 'How could it have been his property?'

'Because his mother owned it and she left it to him.'

'His mother? What are you talking about?'

'Your father's first wife—'

'Our father's what?' Katie shrieked.

'There's no mention of that in your mother's documents,' I said.

'Mama would never have married a divorced man, Catholics can't—'

Mrs Lang sounded amused. 'Look, let me put you out of your misery. Your father did marry before—'

'How can you possibly know that if we don't?' Christina demanded.

'But he didn't have any other children of his own—at least not that I know of. The woman he married was called Pearl—'

'Pearl! You're making this up,' Katie said.

'—and she already had a son when she met

80

your father. His name was Justin. Justin Lang.'

Christina said, 'If this is all true, which of course it can't be, what do you say happened to this Pearl?'

'She was killed in the blitz in 1940.'

'Leaving our father to bring up this child we've never even heard of? I don't believe you, this is all crap,' Christina said, and added, 'Offensive, too. I can't imagine why we're listening to this garbage, you'd really better go now.'

'No, Chris,' Katie said, 'I want to know, what d'you say happened to the little boy then?'

'He'd been evacuated from London when war broke out, he was living in the country and stayed on there. Don't worry, your precious father never had to sully his hands with looking after him. Justin went to boarding school and in the holidays he went back to the people who took him in as an evacuee. He came here very seldom so it's no wonder you forgot his existence, though he remembered yours. But he never felt very welcome here and he only went to Portheglos once.'

'Portheglos! How d'you know about that? Chris, she knows so much about us all, this might all be true after all.'

Marguerite Lang had touched a sensitive nerve. Portheglos is the name of a farm and valley in North Cornwall. I haven't been there for years, though was determined to go back—

as was every other Kittermaster—for the total solar eclipse which would be visible in Cornwall and West Devon, though nowhere else in Britain, at eleven in the morning on 11 August 1999.

Portheglos plays a very special role in the Kittermasters' sense of what they are.

It came into the family by marriage sometime in the eighteenth century and for the next hundred years remained one of those English estates that were held together by primogeniture. Then the last male heir was killed at Passchendaele. Numerous legal machinations later the property had been divided and subdivided amongst the cousins and connections. The house itself, ugly, rambling and never what anyone could have called a stately home, had dwindled (literally, as a wing here and an extension there crumbled and was demolished) into a working farmhouse occupied by a tenant because none of the family wanted to have anything to do with agriculture.

They did however want the outbuildings. Labourers' cottages, barns, boathouses, beach-huts and sheds were all gradually converted into more or less comfortable holiday homes, each owned by different branches of the family, some shared between siblings, others quarrelled over, all passed on from generation unto generation. In August you could go to the small rocky beach and find that everyone on it was more or less distantly related. And—except for the children—nearly all of them were women.

Where were all the men, the fathers? When I was very young mine was the only one who'd disappeared though as time passed and customs changed others were to go off with younger wives or even with other men. Some of 'the Daddies' had to work, teaching summer schools or grabbing the laboratory space in the summer vacation when the competition was less fierce, or staying in 'the office' and 'the city'. Others, like Bertram, went climbing in Scotland and Switzerland or ocean sailing. Even those who put in an appearance at Portheglos kept clear of the beach. Buckets, spades and sandy sandwiches were still women's prerogative in those days, as of course was child minding.

I used to be passed round from aunt to cousin. The analogy is a parcel. Or a hot potato. I don't like to imagine the phone calls my mother must have made, begging/persuading/prevailing upon her relations in turn holiday after school holiday, wishing me on them like a piece of left-luggage. The time I'd been landed on Elena I had to share a room with the girls. They slept in bunk beds and I was on a canvas camp bed, with a kapok sleeping bag. Those were the days when I could still sleep soundly. My memories are patchy but I do remember how uncomfortable it was and that their nappies, double layers of towelling and muslin, smelt equally disgusting on a bottom or in a bucket. By the time Luke was a baby we happily used disposables; *après nous* the environmental consequences.

There was no electricity at Portheglos then, and in Elena's cottage, converted from a coastguard's look-out post, not even a Lister generator, so no television and I wasn't allowed to read in bed in case my candle burnt the cottage down. The lavatory was outside in a wooden shed. You weren't supposed to put anything down it and having only just started my periods in an era when they were never referred to, I didn't know what to do with soiled sanitary towels and was embarrassed to ask; I'll never forget the shame and fear (of discovery) that I felt conducting my secretive burials. It rained. I read my way through a mould-blackened set of the complete works of John Buchan, knitted 'strips' to be sewn into blankets 'for the poor refugees' and in intervals between showers sulkily dragged the little girls out to pick blackberries in the hope of meeting the boy cousins whose family had the old stables. In the evenings Elena taught me how to cook. She had a Calor gas stove and no fridge. There were mouse droppings in the larder. We made goulash and the family speciality of beiglis and—

'Oh heavens,' I exclaimed.

'What is it?' Christina and Katie chorused.

'This Justin, was he very dark, his skin and hair and eyes and all, with a terribly deep voice?'

'He was dark, yes, and he sang bass', Mrs Lang said.

'That must have been him, he was the Star Man! I never knew his name, or maybe I did and completely forgot it. But him—I certainly remember him. He did come to Portheglos that summer I was parked on your mother. He turned up for supper one night and slept on the sofa and left before breakfast. I can see him now, he had black eyes and a fisherman's sweater. I was only about eleven but I thought he was gorgeous.'

'He was a good-looking man,' his widow agreed.

It was vivid in my memory. 'He was the one who told me about astronomy.'

I don't recall how we came to be outside together in the dark. Perhaps we met by torchlight on the way to that insalubrious outside lavatory. Being miles from any streetlights, Portheglos was very dark at night, except when there was a fullish moon.

On one side the rough grass was separated from the cliff top by a low, turf-covered wall. On the inland side there was a five-barred gate into a field where sheep made wuffling noises in the soft night air. Surf broke with a gentle rhythm on the rocks far below. From further away came the soft chug-chug of some other cousin's electricity generator. We leant against the gate and he made me look at the heavenly bodies: stars, constellations, planets. I'd never really noticed them before.

Look properly, he'd said, see, are they all white? D'you see hints of colour, bluish, reddish, there you are. And their shapes. Make patterns, Vicky, like in a dot-to-dot book. A dipper like Elena's milk saucepan, a belt. A face, I suggested. Maybe, he said, or a running man. Or a flower. It was a voyage on a magic carpet.

Then he showed me how to look through his telescope. I could still feel the cold ring of metal and my screwed-up eyes, all these years on. And suddenly white spots popped out of the blackness, a complication of light. Other times, other places, worlds beyond my little patch. The sun's a star too, he'd said.

'He first told me about the sky, the names of stars, the moon and the sun, he talked about eclipses,' I told the girls.

'What about them?' Christina asked.

'How extraordinary they must be, darkness at noon, with birds roosting and all the stars bright as night. He said we'd be able to see it here, in that exact spot where we were standing, when I was forty-nine.' That's a date, he'd said, but I hadn't believed I could ever be that old.

'Stop!' Christina said. 'We've all heard more than enough about that, thanks.' Christina was referring to the blitz of publicity that for months had been foreshadowing the 1999 total eclipse.

'I know, sorry,' I said.

'But go on about your Star Man,' Christina snapped.

'He told me names, lovely words, Andromeda, Pleiades, Alpha Centauri. I remember asking him what a cloud in the night sky was and he said it was the galaxy we live in, billions of stars. The Milky Way. Oh, if that was Justin, he changed my life!'

'Look,' Christina said. 'Even if we accept what you say, if Justin was our father's stepson, how could you be his widow? What happened to him? Where's he been all our lives? When did he die?'

But Mrs Lang looked at her watch and rose to her feet. 'I can't stay now. You've got a lot to learn about your precious father. He wasn't quite the plaster saint you lot want people to think now he's gone.'

'Our father never did a dishonourable thing in his life!' Katie cried, clasping her hands on her heaving bosom.

'Dishonourable, illegal, snobbish—'

'How dare you!' Christina said in a powerful, steady hoot. 'I must ask you to leave now.'

'You always were a fiery little thing—'

'What makes you say that? What d'you know about me?'

87

'Well, my dear,' Mrs Lang said languidly, standing up, knotting her pretty scarf, peering in the cloudy mirror to stroke an eyebrow with the tip of a licked finger, 'we're sort of sisters-in-law, you might say.'

'I might not!' Christina announced firmly.

'You'll see. Read the will and the deeds and the documents. Waste your money on lawyers' bills all you want, but you'll find that everything I've said is true.'

The three of us stood together on the front doorstep and watched the tall, narrow figure disappear towards Kensington High Street. There didn't seem to be anything useful to say. Katie had a deadline and went off to write her column of astrological predictions. Her subject seemed ludicrous to me as an astronomer, even if an amateur one, but I did have to recognise that she was sincere. I'd watched her performing calculations with scientific if misguided care. When the next morning I glanced, wincing, at the paper I couldn't help noticing that her forecasts were full of financial foreboding no matter what the star sign. Virgos could expect troublesome queries about their accounts, Capricorns—like Katie herself—should be careful not to commit themselves to anything they might not be able to afford in the end, while Leos, which Christina was, shouldn't count their chickens before they were hatched.

Christina returned to the death-bed of her

current patient, the husband of a friend. Her unofficial speciality, Christina had once told me, was effecting last-minute reconciliations. Having watched her unconsoling 'counselling' of Elena before she died, I have added a clause to my own 'living will' forbidding Christina or any other of death's self-appointed midwives from coming to utter banalities in my last days. No doubt Christina's own patients are more patient. Or perhaps in *extremis* one changes one's mind.

The sky was blackening and the air felt raw and snow-laden. I set off home before the weather made bicycling too difficult and rang Mr Paxton again from my own flat. He was in the middle of some holiday excursion—his shouts into the mobile phone were interspersed with appeals to his children to shut up—and agreed we'd see Mrs Lang together when he returned and find out more details of her claim. He, being a lawyer, didn't seem in a hurry; I, being an executor longing to be finished with all this, was. 'I'll see you next month then, Mrs Merton, my secretary will fix a time, and meanwhile you might consider asking around. Someone ought to know something about Justin Lang. When I get back I'll check my father's private notebooks and I'd recommend you to speak to your relatives.'

CHAPTER EIGHT

The final three days in China were spent on a mini-cruise on the Yangtse followed by a bus journey for a quick view of the Terracotta Warriors and a hop on Air China ('A.C. stands for Always Crashes,' Hilly whispered to Ari) down to Hong Kong for a shopping opportunity. By the time they boarded the London-bound jet everyone seemed worn out, and Hilly was worried about Mr Feuerstein who though uncomplaining was unwell. She had become quite fond of him. He, the unremittingly awful Mrs Harpner and Ari were the only three of her companions she expected to remember. But the sincere hope that Mr Feuerstein would be all right was not entirely unselfish.

Hilly sat in the middle of a row of three seats with the old man by the window, his eyes closed and his breathing stertorous. Three stewardesses had come by in turn to ask if he was OK. They were afraid there mightn't be a doctor on board. Hilly truthfully assured them Mr Feuerstein had brought a medical certificate from home, as the agency required, saying he'd been fit to travel and there was no reason to think he had contracted a serious condition, he was probably just overtired. But Hilly wasn't as confident as she made herself sound. If he was really ill could he last out to London? If not and he was off-loaded somewhere *en route*, she would have to stay with him. She'd have to make arrangements. Hilly sat neurotically imagining contingencies while Ari, in the aisle seat, worked on his laptop, sorting and annotating the journal he had been keeping throughout the trip.

Mr Feuerstein refused the meal and dozed again. After the movie Hilly dropped off too, waking with a start somewhere over the Middle East. Ari was fast asleep, his jaw dropped. He hadn't shaved for at least three days nor washed his shirt for longer than that. I won't be seeing him again, she thought.

Then Mr Feuerstein needed to be helped to climb out and totter panting along the aisle to the washroom. The cabin lights were off, all its occupants asleep or wishing they were. Having settled the old man down again, Hilly felt wide awake. She sprayed her dry face with spring water from a miniature aerosol can and rubbed salve into her lips. Ari whispered, 'Want a drink?' and pressed his buzzer. He chose cognac, she, for once ignoring the rule of avoiding alcohol on long flights, ordered scotch.

On the last lap of a trip, Hilly often felt able to ask or say things she had been too tactful to utter while she still had to keep her charges happy. She could relax the prohibition on such topics as religion, politics and family history.

91

She still fancied Ari rotten and this might be her last chance to pierce through his reserve.

'Did you say you'd grown up on a kibbutz?' she began. 'Which one was it? I once went to a few of them on a Holy Land tour.'

'Your holy places would hardly have included our kibbutzim.'

Embarrassed, she said quickly, 'Oh, I'm sorry, I didn't mean to suggest—it was just that I wondered—'

'Oh, it's cool, I'm used to it. Anyway you wouldn't have gone within miles of the dump my ma chose to martyr herself in.'

'What d'you mean, chose to—?'

'She had the crazy kind of notions new settlers bring, all that crap about physical labour and discomfort. It's dying out now, but when they arrived, my mum and dad, they landed in one of the worst. I left the moment I could.'

'Is your family still there? I mean, I know you said your father wasn't, but your mother, or have you any brothers or sisters?'

'My mom gave up on the hard labour bit in the end, she's moved to South Africa and lets herself be waited on hand and foot.'

'I've done the Table Mountain and game parks route, it's beautiful, d'you go there often?'

'Not if I can help it.'

'Oh, what a shame, don't you want to? But perhaps being brought up on a kibbutz makes families less close, didn't they design the system on purpose to weaken the parental bond?—I'm being tactless. Sorry.'

'Not much point these days, she's not with it any more.' The stewardess brought the drinks, three miniatures for Ari.

'Is he OK?' the girl asked, looking at Mr Feuerstein.

'I think so, he's asleep anyway,' Hilary murmured.

'He's a bad colour.'

Ari poured the contents of all three little bottles into the plastic tumbler.

'Actually,' Hilly went on, 'you must have been unlucky, I thought the kibbutzim I saw were lovely. So . . . so cooperative.'

'Huh! Real kibbutzim aren't pretty tourist traps like you saw. Ours was in the desert, an aloe farm, bloody hard work, they use Arab labourers now.'

At this point the 'Fasten seat belts' sign was illuminated, with a broadcast announcement about turbulence. Hilly turned to make sure that Mr Feuerstein was properly belted. His breathing was noisy and seemed ever more laboured. His eyes flickered open and he gave a rather ghastly smile before sleeping again.

'So what happened to your father after he left the kibbutz? I know you said you lost touch, but—'

Mr Cohen spoke from across the aisle. 'His father turned into a bloody hero if he was in

93

Mossad.'

'I never said that!' Ari protested.

'A nod's as good as a wink to a—I guessed it. Deduced. Most efficient secret intelligence in the world.' He spoke with an enthusiasm that was not entirely sober. 'Biggest secret ever kept quiet, what they knew in advance about the Six Day War—if he was part of that operation—' Mrs Cohen ostentatiously jabbed her elbow into her husband's midriff and he emitted an injured squawk and subsided.

'I don't know what happened to my pop after he scarpered,' Ari said loudly, and Mr Feuerstein whispered something.

Hilly said, 'Sorry, what did you—?'

'*Aber du solst*. But he should, the boy must honour his father. An—' He rolled the guttural and lengthened the vowels. '*Lebt er noch*? Is he alive?'

Ari seemed startled by the question.

'Lives he still?'

'Answer him,' Hilly hissed.

'Don't ask me,' Ari muttered.

'*Ungeheurt*—monstrous—and you a Jew!'

Ari began to speak but Mr Feuerstein's eyes had fallen closed again. There was a dribble of spittle on his chin, which Hilly wiped gently away. The screened map showed a tiny aeroplane aiming across the Mediterranean. Two more hours. She hoped the old man would last out that long.

94

CHAPTER NINE

The moment one's personally involved, one begins to understand why the law delays. I had to do some work. I needed to see one of the directors of the company I was working for, then there had to be a meeting with some of the other lexicographers, and every such encounter involves careful preparation. Mrs Lang sent a message that she would be abroad, but expected to see some movement on her case by the time she returned in April. Then I got flu, like most of London that spring if the local news was to be believed. The 'welcome death' stage only lasted a few days, though during them I'd have posted a pressing invitation to the man with a scythe if I'd known how. But it took weeks after that to feel like doing anything more taxing than lie round in my flat re-reading Georgette Heyer novels. My neighbour Fidelis Berlin kept me supplied until she went down with the flu herself, after which I made myself go at least as far as the food shop on the corner to get the aspirins and orange juice she needed. And then I got a message that Mr Paxton had gone down with the flu.

I waited to be un-infectious before going to see elderly relatives, beginning, because she was the oldest and I liked her, with Aunt

Connie.

'Justin Lang! My dear, I hadn't heard that name for donkey's years.' Connie's health had deteriorated in the last months. I'd found her with oxygen cylinders beside her chair and a trayful of pills on her table. Her housekeeper warned me not to tire her out. But her mind was not dimmed.

'Have you heard the name recently, then?' I asked.

'That young man of Gayle's mentioned it.'

'Marcus Foster?'

'Yes, he came here to talk about the family. My dear, he's perfectly charming, you must meet him. Writing a book—' Connie's voice was swallowed by the rubber mask she clamped to her face. One hand gestured me to go on talking so I said rather sourly:

'I know. It's about the Kittermasters.'

'He told me it's what keeps the wolf from the door, Gayle's been very generous, apparently, but he's a novelist really.'

'Oh? Any good?'

'I hadn't heard of him.'

'Nor have I.' But I didn't add that I hardly ever read fiction, since I prefer facts to other people's fantasies.

'I have his book on order from the public library,' Connie told me.

'Did Mr Foster mention Bertram?' I asked nervously.

'Oh, all that impertinent nonsense about his

Cambridge friends, all got up by the tabloids—no, dear, of course not, I wouldn't have let him, but he didn't utter a word, nobody's taking that idea seriously. One of our family in the pay of the Russians—the very idea! But haven't you spoken to him yourself yet?'

I replied, 'No, there's not much I could tell him, but he seems to have been in touch with everyone, Gayle's ego trip must be costing a pretty penny.'

'He called our family history his day-job,' Aunt Connie said.

'So what could you tell him about Justin Lang?'

'My dear, absolutely nothing, though I do know he went to the bad, there may have been trouble—drink, drugs, theft, I've no idea what and naturally I didn't say anything about it to Mr Foster. I could easily be wrong.'

'It does seem odd that his existence could be so completely forgotten,' I said.

'Ah, well, in my case it's because I was away.' Aunt Connie had been a GI bride. 'I was in Virginia till 1969, and I wasn't in London during the war either, I joined up, as we all did, dear.' Her eyes were bright and her mind sharp, but talking was difficult. 'My unit was stationed in Scotland. Actually, Bertram was there himself, I met him in the street in Oban when he was coming off a ferry from the islands and I was getting on one, so you could say we passed in the night.'

'What was he doing?'

'Oh my dear, one was always very careful not to inquire, nearly everyone was in one hush-hush job or another. And I didn't see him again, or any of the cousinage for that matter, it was more than twenty years.'

Connie now had wispy white hair scraped over a pink skull. Her face was a mesh of fine lines and her slackened lips and hooded eyelids quivered. But I'd seen pictures of Connie as a girl. She looked delicious then, with semicircular eyes and shining rolls of hair and a softly rounded figure which must have been irresistible in uniform. Too busy to have time for boring old relations. And at that time, before the war, Bertram was working abroad.

I asked, 'Do you know anything about Justin Lang's mother, Bertram's first wife? She seems to have been written out of the history books too.'

Between gulps of oxygen she gasped out what she remembered. It took a long time.

'I'd heard he'd got married, there were jokes about it.'

'Jokes?'

'Well, dear, she was a foreigner of some sort, he'd brought her back from abroad, at least I think he did. D'you know, I could be imagining that, though I certainly remember hearing she was Jewish, that set the cat among the—oh, my dear, I'm sorry,' she added, remembering too late that my father had been an American Jew, 'don't take it personally, but we were all disgustingly insular in those days.'

'And anti-Semitic.'

'My dear, I am sorry to say that lots of people were at the time.'

Although I'm still a determined agnostic and can't understand how anyone could be anything else, who looks at the night sky and realises the magnitude of the universe, I do know more about Judaism than I used to, after sitting in on Fidelis's Hebrew lessons. But I never thought of myself as Jewish even when I was at school and the other girls did; and they showed it. A lot of the parents who sent their daughters there were narrow-minded and ignorant. It was years before anyone dreamt of legislation about race relations, and jibes and jokes were common currency. I was often told Jews were mean; they used 'Jewy', meaning grasping, as an adjective and 'to Jew' as a verb. In those people's minds Shylock was 'a Jew-boy' and stood for a whole people. Perhaps because I was a Kittermaster in my mind, not a Moss, I managed never to believe the prejudice really applied to me. Or perhaps I should say I subconsciously tried to ensure it wouldn't, always giving away my sweets and refusing repayment of loaned pocket money. The world has changed and by the time I'm describing now, Aunt Connie's careless words should have provoked anger, if anything. Instead I felt a surge of that old familiar shame.

'It's all such a long time ago,' Connie murmured apologetically and, as I'd always automatically done, I cringed inwardly but passed over the offence as though I hadn't noticed it.

'Bertram worked abroad before the war, they said at his memorial, does that mean he met this Pearl in China or America, do you know?'

'My dear, how can I tell after all this time? But of course we all thought he was in the secret service in those days,' Connie whispered.

'Really? I thought he was a doctor.'

'He was doing some kind of research into germs, we knew that—well, after he got the prize the whole world knew that. But . . . wait a moment.' She sucked urgently at the artificial air.

'Should I fetch someone?' I asked, but she waved one hand, gesturing for me to stay where I was. The room was close and dry, two bars of a wall-mounted electric fire blazing out too much heat. It used to be the sitting-room, but Connie's bed had been moved downstairs into it and stood against the wall on which hung the famous Sargent portrait of Connie's American mother, all creamy flesh and velvet folds. Connie was rich, but her room could have been labelled 'It'll see me out.' Nothing had been replaced just for the fun of it, although the serviceable furniture and fittings

100

were in good condition, unlike Elena's.

'There must have been family gossip about Pearl, surely?'

'It's no use, Vicky, I just don't remember. Bertram was never—d'you understand what I mean if I say he was never at the heart of the family? Even before he got so famous. I really hardly knew him, he didn't even come to Portheglos. Of course we were proud of him, and after he won the Nobel prize one couldn't help being aware of him, he was so famous. I always thought Elena was a dear good soul but she had a hard time of it with him, I fear.' This speech, interrupted by struggles for breath, had taken ages, with me sitting there nodding and smiling and trying to look as though my understanding was as slow as poor Connie's speech.

'A hard time?' I prompted.

'Bertram can't have been easy to live with, geniuses never are—even when he was young my mother used to say he was churlish. No social graces, you know, my dear? But of course he had to concentrate on his work, I can see that now. And of course he was a few years older than me, so even if he hadn't been slaving away in laboratories all the time he'd never have been in our set before the war.'

'But after that you must have heard something, in a family like ours, didn't you? My mum always said there was a kind of tomtom spreading any news.' I stopped myself saying more, suddenly remembering that Connie herself had been one of the usual repositories and disseminators of information.

She said, 'All I knew was that Pearl had been caught in an air raid.'

'And her son?'

'Bertram must have taken the boy on, but really, my dear, I don't recall anything about it. By the time I came home again he'd been married to Elena for years, she got out of Hungary in '56 you know, and I'd see her maybe once a year, and the boy was never mentioned that I remember. When I saw her Bertram wasn't ever there, too busy, and he—' She was interrupted by a bout of coughing, at which a woman in nurse's uniform came in and told me to leave.

*   *   *

The next step was to ring some of those I knew among the other aunts and uncles, as all senior relations were collectively known, though some were no more than third or fourth cousins. You would have thought there would still be lots of people to remember the forties and fifties in an extended family the size of ours but memory is famously selective and people who'd been schoolchildren or students at the time were not then interested in irrelevant relations, however gossipy they became later. But I did expect those born

102

earlier in the century to be more helpful.

The first one I tried was a non-starter, for it turned out that he'd descended rapidly into Alzheimer's since I caught sight of him at Bertram's funeral. The next was away on a sponsored bike ride along the Nile. Number three had been rubber planting in Malaya until he was imprisoned by the Japanese; he had no idea what his distant cousins had been up to back home. With number four, Uncle Edgar Kittermaster, who had been a patent lawyer, I thought I'd hit pay dirt. I had to explain who I was—Sheila's daughter, Felix's granddaughter —and what I wanted. The television was on in the background. He'd been watching *East-Enders*.

'Are you working with that young fellow of your cousin Gayle's?'

'Her writer? No, I'm not.'

'In that case why are you asking the same questions?'

'Did he ask about Justin Lang? I didn't realise.'

'Dragging it all up . . .' Uncle Edgar sounded at once weary and angry.

'Dragging what up? I don't quite understand.'

'You're making trouble, Victoria, leave this alone.'

'Couldn't I come and talk to you? I could explain why we need to—'

'No.'

'Only when it's a convenient time for you, of course.'

'I can't discuss it.'

'But—

'The subject is closed.'

'Sorry, I don't understand . . .'

Incredibly, he put the phone down on me, a disconcerting thing to happen. Nobody had ever hung up on me before. Whatever had that been about? I reminded myself to ask Gayle how to get in touch with 'her writer'. Meanwhile, telling myself that Edgar probably had Alzheimer's too, I called the last name on my list—Aunt Charity, born 1918. Her son Peter answered. I'd never heard of him nor he of me, which, given that we must have been second cousins once removed, did rather go to show how little his own generation might have known about Uncle Bertram's first marriage or stepson. Charity was past understanding, and Peter knew nothing about Justin Lang or Pearl Kittermaster. He said:

'If you're checking on a marriage, there are public records for that, look it up, why don't you?'

Why didn't I? Why, indeed, hadn't I? It was the obvious thing to do, so the next day I ran the gauntlet of half a dozen teenagers congregated outside the house and walked up to the Tube station. I won't go into detail about the process that followed of trying to find the right information at the Registrar

General's office for Births Marriages and Deaths. I had not realised that such details were no longer researched among shelves of leatherbound documents at Somerset House, but that this office had long since moved from there and even from its next home in St Catherine's House. Having trailed uselessly round London for hours I finally finished up at Myddelton Street where I did find archives of names but was told it was going to take days to get hold of copies of detailed certificates, which had to be requested and paid for in advance. But I left without ordering anything.

It was a surprise to find that Kittermaster is not at all an unusual name. Casting my net wide I looked in the years between 1935 and 1945 and found that dozens of them had got married, not one with the initial B or to a woman called Lang. Nor, anywhere in the 1980s (yes, it all took hours, in case you were wondering), did I find any record of the death of a Justin Lang. This—and please note the word-play—was a dead end.

CHAPTER TEN

Hilly hovered uncertainly at a distance before the service began and then edged in as unobtrusively as she could and sat at the very back. She saw that she needn't have bothered with black clothes and a hat. Most people were in anoraks or tweeds and few of the women had covered their heads though all of the men did, many of them with small black trilbies, and even Ari had attached a yarmulka to his slippery black hair with a kirby grip.

Hilly had found his London number in the travel company's computer and summoned up the courage to ring him. But he did not even recognise her name until she mentioned poor Mr Feuerstein and then it clicked. But he'd not sounded very interested. Now, unexpectedly, here he was, looking perfectly at home in the chapel at Golders Green Crematorium. The only other time Hilly had been there it had been for a Christian service and it had not occurred to her that the religious symbols were less permanent than in other churches, but for this service the crucifix, banners and altar had been hidden away, to be replaced with what Hilly assumed were Jewish symbols. The service was in Hebrew. Hilly read the translation on a laminated page. It didn't seem so different from what she was used to, except for the suggestion that immortality resided in the memory left behind rather than the future of the soul.

Ari did not join in as the other mourners murmured and sang, but he stood there in a kind of amenable co-operation that Hilly wouldn't have expected of him. Come on, she told herself, what did you think he'd do, break

106

it all up, make some kind of rude scene? No; what she had expected was that he wouldn't come.

Maybe, just maybe, he'd actually wanted to see her again? She fell in beside him as the room emptied, both hanging back from the tribe to which they were outsiders. He said:

'Shouldn't you be off on a trip somewhere? I thought you spend your life travelling.'

'I only do a dozen or so a year. There's Patagonia next month, the Baltic, the Blue Train through Southern Africa and the Garden Route in the Cape.'

'Way to go.'

It was chilly with a vicious, gusting, dust-laden wind; a bleak early-summer day and a bleak occasion. 'It's a shame, he was a nice old man. Apparently he went downhill fast after we got back. At least he did what he wanted.' She repeated the trite comfort to some middle-aged mourners, presumably the next generation of Feuersteins. 'At least he fulfilled his ambition.'

'And he'd still be alive if he hadn't, China of all places,' a sharp-faced woman snapped. 'That ridiculous obsession with family history—I told him it would kill him in the end and so it did.'

'Now, Becky, you know what it meant to him,' a softer-looking man said. 'The body can be killed but the memory must live on, that's what he always said.'

Hilly had thought, but not dared hope, that Ari might not leave straight away, and tried not to let her pleasure show when he hailed a taxi and said, 'Coming?' Jolting along the grey streets, she tried not to stare at him. He'd removed the skull cap, but still wore an unfamiliar dark jacket over a clean white T-shirt. His eyes glistened like black olives. Hilly's tan had faded but he was still a glossy amber. It must be the natural colour of his skin. You wouldn't ever marry someone like that. Anyway Hilly wanted to marry a banker or chartered surveyor and live in an old rectory. But think of the fun you could have with someone so different. A foreigner. An academic. She'd never had a boyfriend who was circumcised.

'I'm going to Clapham, where d'you want?' he said.

Hilly lived far west, in Ealing, but said, 'Oh, I'm going south of the river too.'

She put forward conversational feelers. Their trip in China, Mr Feuerstein's family, the weather, the traffic jam they were stuck in.

Ari was restless, hunting for things in his pockets, tying and retying his shoe laces, leaning forward to read the small print of the advertisements on the jump seat. He took off his coat, spilled coins and credit cards from its inside pocket and grovelled for them on the floor.

'Awful for Mr Feuerstein's family,' Hilly

said.

'Yeah.'

'It makes you think. I don't see enough of my parents, one ought to while they're—well, you know.'

Ari was unforthcoming.

'Didn't you say you had family in South Africa?' Hilly persisted. She felt the tense arm beside hers relaxing. He drawled:

'Yup, my mother.'

'How long's she lived there? I mean, she's an Israeli, right?'

'Actually she was born in Bradford.'

'Oh.'

'Melting pot's the expression you're looking for. Israel's a—et cetera.'

'Would you like me to take her anything when I'm there?'

'That would be good,' he said with a pleased smile, adding as an afterthought, 'If you wouldn't mind.'

'No, it's cool,' Hilly said, realising it would mean seeing him again.

'Great, I'll be in touch then.'

'Couldn't you do with a drink after that funeral?'

'Nah, I don't have time, I'll split here. See you. Driver, I'm getting out.' The driver pulled on his handbrake to release the handle and Ari jumped between three columns of cars to the pavement. Hilly watched him, bouncing along in his trainers between the crowds of shoppers.

The lights changed and the cab moved twenty yards. Suddenly she saw he'd failed to pick something up that must have fallen out of his pocket, a computer floppy. Through the rear window she saw Ari disappear from sight through the doors of a shoe shop. Should she return it? Yes, she should, but no, she wouldn't, this might make a useful excuse for seeing him again. She leant forward and tapped on the glass. 'Drop me at the Tube station, please, I don't need to go to Clapham after all. Sorry about that.'

From the *Kensington and Chelsea Chronicle*, April 1999

Police investigating the murder of an oriental male, whose skeleton was found under the patio of a house in Addison Road, are still pursuing their inquiries. Inspector Strange of Notting Hill police station said, 'We are looking at the missing persons lists from forty years ago. We expect to identify these remains sooner or later. Murder is a crime no matter how long ago it occurred.'

CHAPTER ELEVEN

He seemed old for a policeman now that so many startle me by their youth, but also because it's become a job from which people retire early, so it was a long time since I'd seen one who looked so like the old-fashioned archetype of the village bobby. He had a squadron-leader style moustache and neat little grey beard to balance the bare dome of his scalp and he was overweight and unfit. In spite of the high-tech gear dangling from every button and buckle, this was no go-getting sophisticate. I guessed he'd been handed the kind of assignment they saved for officers working out their time.

Another uncharacteristic detail was his candour. In detective dramas on TV they never tell the people they are taking evidence from exactly what the police already know and want to know. But about this ancient crime there seemed to be no secret. The man (and apparently they could be pretty sure the skeleton had been a man's) had been battered to death with the proverbial blunt instrument sometime after 1958, since a coin of that year lay under the bones, and before 1962 when the estate was completed, with all the concrete poured over the patio areas of the new houses.

'D'you mean he was killed somewhere near

by, near here—oh, I can't bear to think of it! And then buried on the old bomb site? Is that what you think?' Katie wailed.

'But that can't be right, surely it would have been dug up when they laid out the new estate,' I said.

DC Hicks replied, 'We guess the body was buried after much of the building work was complete and just before the patios were laid.'

'That could be right, I suppose, but it would have had to be someone who knew how the building was progressing,' I said.

'One of the workmen maybe?' Katie asked, and I went on:

'Or a neighbour. I can just remember it myself, we'd see the new houses growing when we came to visit.'

'Do you, madam?' He turned to me with interest.

'I was twelve in 1962. My mother and I came up to London in the holidays occasionally and used to visit my uncle and aunt here.'

'Up from the country,' he said approvingly.

'You're a countryman yourself, I can sense it,' Katie interrupted. She didn't need to sense it for Constable Hicks had never lost a defining West Country burr, but he seemed quite happy to be diverted on to the subject of Somerset twenty-five years ago, London life and his star sign.

In films people carry on with whatever they

were doing when the policeman calls. No doubt it's thought more watchable if the suspect aims at clay pigeons or scrubs her floor during the official questions, though it never looks very likely. But I'd found it a relief to be interrupted, having been trying and utterly failing to convince Katie that it was time to move out of Addison Road. I knew it couldn't possibly be sold until its ownership was established and, whatever Mr Paxton told us when we met, one thing I knew he'd say was that it might take years. Meanwhile nobody was going to spend any money on it, but the house was in a dismal state, with empty, echoing rooms and an atmosphere that made even me feel bad vibes. Katie perversely, passionately, pointlessly claimed it was her home and she'd jolly well stay for as long as it took. Christina was fed up with the whole thing, had raised a loan on the strength of her expectations and was planning to spend the summer at Portheglos. I was counting the days till August when I could join her. The date of the total eclipse had been engraved on my heart for ages, but since, more recently, the media realised it was due, there were daily reminders to excite me further.

The Addison Road kitchen was even gloomier now than it had seemed in winter. Nobody had trimmed the weeds and brambles which now obscured such little daylight as the ground level windows should let into the basement, more tiles had fallen from the walls, and grime had settled into crannies and corners. Katie didn't seem to wash up very often. The big room was like I'd imagine a badger's underground lair.

I made 'tea' using the only ingredients I could find, which turned out to be a choice of camomile or something called Red Kooga. Constable Hicks sipped heroically.

I interrupted Katie's discourse on the planets alleged to govern the policeman's star sign to ask him what he'd actually come for.

'There's still a few families resident in the same houses, like yourselves.'

'My mother and father might have been able to help you,' Katie said.

'That would be Sir Bertram Kittermaster.'

'And my mother. She died last year.'

'But they were here at the time?'

'Oh yes, my father had lived here since before the war, and Mama came when they got married, that was 1957. And of course she knew lots of the neighbours, she could have told you what went on round here, but I was practically a babe in arms.'

I said, 'I didn't visit very often either, though I can remember the road before they built the new houses, I used to ride round the block on a fairy bike.'

'Not alone?' he asked disapprovingly.

'Don't you remember, children did in those days.'

'It wasn't right, even then,' he said.

There was no point in arguing about historical fact. I said, 'Well, I did anyway, I'd go along beside the "bombsite" as it was called, all one word. I don't think I knew what it meant. Actually it was a piggery. Or—can it have been? Come to think of it, I can't say I remember any pigs. I've got a picture in my mind of a big area, fenced off and quite a bit lower than the road, all rubble and broken earth—yellow—why do I think it was yellow?'

'London clay can look yellowish,' he confirmed.

'Yes, and there was that pink flower that grew in all the bomb sites, rosebay willow herb. But were there really pigs?'

'I believe an old man moved in towards the end of the war and kept one or two. There may have been chickens. They'd have been glad of the extra during rationing. But the permissions had been granted for the new development by 1957.'

'But you said it wasn't finished till years after that.'

'1962. Things moved slowly in those days.'

The phone rang and Katie embarked on a conversation about the future. Not, I mean, where or when to have lunch with her caller, but whether it would be propitious to meet for lunch at all. And other prophecies. I found it extraordinarily irritating to hear her misuse the names of those impersonal stars and

116

planets. Capricorn, Virgo, Cygnus. I wrenched my attention away and said to the policeman:

'D'you believe this man was murdered by someone who lived near by? I mean, the kind of people who could afford houses here—it doesn't seem very likely, surely.'

'Don't you think so, madam?'

I could feel myself blushing. 'No, you're quite right, that was a daft thing to say.' I paused, trying both to close my ears to Katie's sacrilege ('Mercury in the ascendant') and to visualise what might have happened.

Night-time. Streetlights weren't so bright then and there wouldn't have been much traffic. I had a momentary vision of myself at eighteen, Elena's lodger for the nine months between leaving school before Christmas and going up to Cambridge in October. I'd walk from the Tube to Addison Road, briskly along the main road, and not meeting anyone's eyes because, even in 1968, girls didn't feel entirely safe all alone in London at night. And once I turned off into the side road, it was dim and lonely. One reeled in and threw a dwindling or lengthening shadow between successive lamp-posts; and behind the garden fences at the middle point murders could have been committed unnoticed.

('Mars in Jupiter's's house.')

'Is there any way to tell who he was—the victim, I mean?'

'We know it was an oriental man, middle-

117

aged, quite short. The excavators found some hair—black going grey—and complete dentition but for one gold tooth. American dentistry, it's thought.'

'And DNA material to cross-check,' I contributed.

'Of course, if there's anything to cross-check with.'

'Didn't anything he was wearing survive?'

'Tests are still being carried out,' he said evasively.

'What could you tell from them if there is anything?'

'You'd be surprised, madam, what the scientists can do these days.'

Katie had finished her conversation but I didn't think her contribution to this one was much improvement. She offered to *sense* the missing information. 'Anyone who died in distress and terror, as that poor man must have, there'd be emanations, things you might not realise, officer, any more than my cousin would, but I am sure I could help you. Poor man. Poor unquiet soul.'

CHAPTER TWELVE

I haven't been perfectly candid with you. I've lied by omission. It was true to say that my domestic nest emptied out in the same year

118

that I parted from Stuart but I failed to include an important detail: the reason Luke went.

Stuart did get religion, just as I've described, and he really was offered a curacy in the north. He made it very clear that it was out of self-abnegation and consideration for me, because I worked in Oxford, that he hesitated to accept it. He was prepared to stay there, frustrated, on my account. For the sake of our marriage.

Who can really explain even their own motives? Perhaps because of the changes in him, or maybe because of my hostility to his new commitment, I had an affair. It didn't last long, it didn't work, it was not a happy experience, but during that time Stuart left and Luke left with him, giving up the place he'd been offered at The University of Reading and getting himself on to a philosophy course at Liverpool instead.

Luke would not speak to me, even to tell me why not. Was he being loyal to his father? Was he disgusted by the idea of his mother being sexually active? Had he just realised he hated me? I simply cannot tell. All I know is that he didn't want any more to do with me, however much his father preached Christian forgiveness at him. When Stuart told Luke that I had breast cancer he said I was putting it on. I wonder whether he'd have come round if I'd really had it. (In both senses: had cancer, and 'had it', i.e. was doomed.)

You need to know about Luke's hostility

(hatred? affront? jealousy?) towards me if only to understand why he plays so little part in this story. But it also occurs to me that nobody who has met me since I moved to London would know I had a child. If I don't mention him other people don't remember he exists. Neither Elena nor her daughters seem to, for he's never been mentioned in Addison Road. Perhaps the silence about Justin isn't all that unlikely after all.

But Luke's defection had another effect on me. I've become idiotically frightened of boys and young men. I know it's silly but I can't think myself back into the person who dealt happily with hordes of visiting friends. In those days I knew how to talk to them as they lounged on my sofa or kitchen chairs and scoffed my food and drink. But I've forgotten how to make contact with them now, which is why I'm so careful not to provoke my yobbo neighbours. How can I put it? Perhaps to say that I've lost the ear for their talk, or that my waveband has shifted. They now seem like an alien species, and a threatening one. There's no objective reason to suppose they are hostile to me, but I'd really hate those lounging youths to discover my weaknesses. If they knew how scared I am of spiders, how squeamish about blood or bodily fluids . . . well, best to make sure they never know.

It's another thing I'm not proud of. I can still see the scorn and impatience on Stuart's face, not long before things went finally wrong between us. All our married lives he'd been indulgent about my weaknesses. We had an implicit deal. I sewed his buttons on and he took spiders out of the bath. I didn't despise him for being clumsy, he accepted my phobias.

Then one day, he told me not to be so silly, it was about time I pulled myself together, grew up. And that was the moment I suddenly realised that he didn't love me any more.

I've learnt to cope with spiders, though there are other irrational fears I haven't mastered yet, a list of which would only begin with 'rough boys' and go on to include a comprehensive range whose common factor is what you might call *real life*, something I have tended to edge past, eyes averted. 'Think you're too good for the likes of us,' a beggar woman once jeered after me, and maybe you think she hit the nail on the head, but she didn't. It's just that I keep my head down. 'You've never lived,' Stuart accused. Well, I told him, you should know.

It never occurred to me that looking into Marguerite Lang's claim was going to change my life. I offered to do it when we met in the solicitor's office. I'd arrived late and flustered after an uncomfortable call from Cousin Gayle, who had unerringly chosen to ring at the moment I was leaving the flat with my hands full of bag, briefcase, milk-bottle carrier and the garbage. It was one of those viciously

121

windy days when even double glazing doesn't seem to keep the draughts out and grit is hurled against the windows with disconcerting cracking noises. I put the bags down, pulled off my gloves and reached the receiver just as the tape switched on.

I thought Gayle was ringing in reply to my message about the writer she'd commissioned, so was taken aback when she started right in on telling me to lay off. 'I've altered his contract, more money for less work, one didn't want to alienate him, so he's writing the history of my firm now and not about the whole family.' That'll make a short book, I thought, and asked why. 'I just thought it was best,' she said evasively.

'Was he uncovering scandals?' I asked and she snapped back:

'What makes you say that?'

'Nothing, a joke', I said.

'Have you been talking to Uncle Edgar?'

'He wouldn't talk to me.'

I could hear the dustmen in the street outside. Damn, missed them. I went on:

'But listen, Gayle, I just wonder if Marcus Foster might have found anything else about Uncle Bertram and his—'

'Uncle Bertram! What are you talking about?'

How oddly Gayle was behaving—oddly enough to make me suppose there was some substance to my light suggestion of family scandals. If so, she wasn't having any. I did ask if she'd ever heard of Bertram being married before Elena, or anything about a stepson, and she said no. Gayle had been a bad actress when we were kids and still was, I could tell she was pretending though I couldn't think why. What did she know that we didn't? So then I told her I planned to have a word with the writer, because he might have come across something before she called him off, and Gayle said she didn't have his address handy just now, she wasn't sure where he was. I recognised the mulish note in her voice. Nowadays, with her being successful as a captain of industry and commerce the adjective should probably be authoritative, but forty years ago that tone went with a jutting lower lip and braced legs. Nobody had ever made Gayle do anything she didn't want to do or stopped her doing what she wanted. I heard the clock on her mantelpiece chime and realised she wasn't ringing from the open plan office but was in private, at home in the eight-bedroomed house in Cumberland Terrace she'd bought when her business boomed. I could visualise her, as clearly as if we had television-phone. She'd be dressed in black, sitting on one of the three matching white sofas beside an elaborate, all-white flower arrangement which a contractor supplied three times a week, the scene's only colour coming from the impressive Kandinsky a designer had decreed for the wall above the great marble chimneypiece.

I was late. I said I had to rush, left the garbage and milk bottles and ran out into the street where, mercifully, there was a taxi and no neighbours, so I got to Wootton Hardman only a few minutes late, though (being usually on the dot) as hassled as if it were hours.

The girls were waiting for me, and we were ushered into a small conference room to listen with varying degrees of attention and understanding to the legal explanation (justification? excuse?) for the firm's lapse. Nobody used the word negligence.

Mr Paxton was careful to disclaim responsibility. 'This firm didn't act for Sir Bertram until 1961.'

'What's the date of his will?'

'Some years later, 1973.'

'Was that his first one?' Christina asked.

'I have no record of another, but it wasn't myself that dealt with it, you understand, I didn't join the firm till some years later.'

'So he made a will—his last one?'

'Yes, it was never altered, everything was gifted to Lady Kittermaster outright. You understand there were estate duty considerations, transfers between spouses are exempt.'

'And the house? The title deeds?'

'They weren't here, never had been.'

'Wouldn't a prudent lawyer have inquired?'

124

Mr Paxton looked severe. 'Sir Bertram saw my father, who was very highly regarded, Mrs Merton, I can assure you.'

'I'm sure he was, I didn't mean to—'

'My father sadly passed on five years ago, but there's a note in the file. Sir Bertram came by recommendation from Lord Wilson—'

'The politician?'

'The former Prime Minister, yes, Lord Wilson of Rievaulx.'

'But who was his lawyer before that, he must have had one?' Christina asked.

'Not for many years, it seems. There had been a firm called Peters which dealt with his affairs.' His voice took on a disdainful note. 'It was a little local concern in West London, a one-man firm.'

'Unlike this,' Katie murmured. She was standing by the window looking down to the sodden, traffic-jammed streets of the City of London. This glass and steel palace was entirely occupied by Wootton Hardman whose brochure listed the names of ninety-seven partners, several of whom, according to newspaper financial pages, had seven-figure incomes.

'Yes, well, I've made inquiries at the Law Society and it seems their buildings and records were destroyed in the war. A direct hit apparently. The firm disappeared at that time, so we can only suppose that the title deeds to 447 Addison Road were in its safe and went up

125

in smoke along with everything else at that time.'

'That's just not good enough,' Christina said firmly.

'It would have been registered land, surely,' I said, having by then done some research and discovered that in London all land had been compulsorily registered throughout this century. 'The title must have been listed at the Land Registry if they bought the house in the thirties.'

'Yes.' Mr Paxton took out a starched white handkerchief, shook out its folds and wiped his forehead. 'Yes, it was. But nobody—that is to say, we never checked. You have to understand that there wasn't any occasion to do so, we knew the property was unencumbered, though naturally when it changed hands we would have had to—'

'But the house did change hands,' I said relentlessly. 'Elena inherited it.'

'Of course we would have regularised the position in due course, when the estate was finally wound up.'

'So what you're telling us is that nobody checked the register,' Christina said.

'No.'

'And now?'

'Now we have had the opportunity to make the requisite inquiries.' He stopped again.

'Which revealed . . . ?' I pressed.

He mopped his reddened face again. 'This

is all very awkward. Of course the position wouldn't have changed if we'd had the information sooner and indeed it might have made Lady Kittermaster's last months very uncomfortable, I might go so far as to say it's really all to the good that we left well alone . . .'

He paused and Christina said grimly:

'Go on, spit it out.'

'Well, I'm afraid the facts are these. 447 Addison Road was purchased at a knock-down price in 1939, when most people were getting out of London at the beginning of the war. It was sold by a Mr Begby.'

Christina had lost patience. 'To whom was it sold? Do get on with it.'

His voice sounded reluctant, as though the information was being dragged out of him by torture. 'To a Mrs Erica Pearl Lang.'

He'd led up to this announcement so slowly that it was no surprise to any of us.

'She must have bought it before she and father got married,' Katie murmured, and Christina said briskly:

'OK, so she died and her widower inherited, that doesn't change anything, it still became my father's property.'

'Did she leave a will?' Katie asked in a dreamy voice.

'Or did that go up in smoke too?' I suggested.

'I can only assume so,' Mr Paxton said. He looked a little more cheerful now, with the end of his ordeal in sight. 'Sir Bertram—or Mr Kittermaster, he'd have been then, of course—obviously believed himself to have become the beneficial owner of the property at the time.'

'This Marguerite Lang claims Justin's mother left him the house,' Christina said.

'Then presumably she must have some documentary evidence.' Paxton was getting less fraught by the minute, comforted by the prospect of paper and signatures.

Prompt to the cue, the intercom buzzed. 'Mrs Lang's here, Mr Paxton.'

'Good. Show her in.'

We waited in awkward silence. Our meeting was not in Mr Paxton's own office, which might have displayed some such personal touches as family photos or a sporting trophy Instead we were in a small, airless 'conference room' furnished like a dining-room, with pads and pencils instead of plates and cutlery, and a sideboard on which was a vase of artificial flowers and a tray of up-market cups and vacuum jugs. There was a small, dull seascape on one wall and, I noticed, a panic button just behind the chair Mr Paxton had chosen. Violently angry clients must be an occupational hazard. That one-man outfit in West London would have had lower overheads, I thought, wondering how much of the several-million-pound estate would be left to inherit after Wootton Hardman's generous cut.

When Mrs Lang came in, the girls both stayed grumpily and silently where they were but Mr Paxton and I stood up to greet her.

She was wearing a stone-coloured trouser suit, carried a tan leather briefcase and looked serenely confident. She sat at the table, facing me and the girls, clicked open the case and produced a sheaf of papers. One was a document attested in English and Hebrew by an attorney from Tel Aviv, the record of a legal marriage in 1961 between Marguerite Goldsmith and Justin Lang. 'Our generation of immigrants usually took Hebrew names, so he changed his name after that, but actually he did it quite often depending where he moved to but he never did it legally and we weren't ever divorced,' she said. 'When he died he was going by the name Luis Gomez.'

One by one, she passed over Luis Gomez's death certificate (Pretoria, 1986), the birth certificate of Justin Amadeus Lang, born June 1930 in the Duchess of Connaught Nursing Home, Peak View, Hong Kong, son of Pearl nee Steimatsky and Jacob Lang; a certificate of a marriage that took place in the British Consulate in Harbin in June 1929: Pearl Steimatsky to Jacob Lang. Another marriage certificate: Pearl Lang, widow, to Bertram Kittermaster, Hong Kong, 1939.

'Well, that's straightforward enough,' I said.

Then, with the air of a conjurer, Marguerite drew out another document. It attested a death in the absence of a conventional certificate: Jacob Lang, in Japanese-occupied North China in May or June 1943. This document was sworn by an American pastor, who signed himself as a member of the Baptist Missionary Society, and witnessed by a medical doctor, ditto.

'I don't understand,' Katie said plaintively. 'Who are these people?'

'Jacob Lang was Pearl's first husband,' I said, and Christina told her savagely:

'Idiot, don't you see, it means she was a bigamist, she was never legally married to Father.'

'But that's good, isn't it?' Katie innocently asked.

'Oh, Katie, for God's sake—'

'Perhaps she got a divorce,' I suggested.

'In which case she'd hardly have described herself as a widow, would she?' Christina demanded.

'I still don't get it.' Katie sounded aggrieved. 'What was Father doing in China anyway?'

'He did some work there before the war, they said so at his funeral,' I reminded her.

'Nobody can blame our father for being deceived by this woman. He was certainly never a knowing bigamist,' Christina said.

Mr Paxton made the gesture of pulling the meeting to order. He put the documents down on the table in front of him and said, 'Let's be clear. Your assertion, Mrs Lang, is that in the absence of a legal marriage to Pearl Lang, Sir Bertram Kittermaster could not inherit her property on an intestacy and the house in Addison Road consequently devolved upon her son Justin?'

'My late husband. Yes.'

'Are you saying this—this person can suddenly turn up out of the blue and take our home away?' Katie wailed, forgetting that she had not lived there during most of her adult life.

Christina said coldly, 'After all these years? You can't suddenly come along and say we hadn't any right to be there.'

And I asked, 'What about squatters' rights? Fifty years should be long enough.'

'The question of acquiring title by adverse possession's always an interesting one,' Mr Paxton said, but Marguerite Lang spoke over him.

'Maybe, but it does depend on Justin not asserting his rights.'

Paxton and Christina spoke together. 'How d'you know that?' 'That's correct.'

Marguerite said calmly, 'As it happens, unfortunately for you, Bertram Kittermaster—'

'Sir Bertram to you,' Christina hissed.

'—knew perfectly well that the house was Justin's property. Justin made a point from the very beginning of writing to remind him of it. Notes, cards, messages. You may not have seen them but that changes nothing.'

131

'He did, I found some,' I cried, suddenly remembering the cards I'd chucked out into plastic rubbish sacks. 'They were rather obscure messages, weren't they? You'd have to know what they were about.' *Keep the home fires burning*, one had said; another promised, *Back soon*. One had set up some kind of appointment. They were still in the attic, I hadn't got round to carrying the rubbish downstairs.

'They were about reminding Bertram Kittermaster that he occupied that house on licence,' Marguerite said with a kind of savagery, her teeth showing more in a snarl than a smile.

'Well, why didn't he jolly well say so, then? After all these years—it's not right,' Katie wailed.

'Where was he anyway, what happened to him?' I asked.

The intercom spoke again. Mr Paxton's next client was waiting. Like a judge closing the evidence and argument he drew a firm line under his scribbled notes.

'This can't be resolved quickly,' he pronounced.

'But what do we do meanwhile? There's the house half packed up, there's buyers coming to see it—' Christina protested.

'It will have to be taken off the market for the time being. There will need to be investigations.'

132

'I quite understand that,' Mrs Lang agreed. 'Meanwhile I expect my expenses to be paid by the estate.'

'I shall have to seek counsel's opinion,' Mr Paxton said, escorting us four women to the lift. I went back to Addison Road in a cab with Katie.

The house seemed unutterably dismal. Any prospective purchaser would have to have a very imaginative eye to see past the increasing grime, the spreading damp and the general atmosphere of abandonment that prevailed in spite of Katie having taken up possessive residence in the basement. I wasn't keen to excavate the rubbish sacks I'd filled so many weeks ago but it had to be done. I went up the echoing stairs to the attic, and the first thing my eye fell on was Elena's incomprehensible diary which I'd put aside and forgotten about. This needed to be translated right away, and I put it in my bag. Then, squeamishly, I began on the bags of paper.

Sod's law operated as usual. I tried to cheat it by varying the order, but of course the cards had to be in the very last bag I untied and emptied out on the floor. I found half a dozen postcards in the tiny handwriting I remembered. If there had also been letters which survived they would now be with Bertram's other correspondence in the United States.

Shovelling the discarded documents back

into the rubbish sack, I just glanced at every sheet to make sure the same handwriting didn't appear, and did come across one more card caught on a paper clip behind a couple of newspaper cuttings. The card read, *You know where I am if you need me.* The cutting was about the skeleton found on a former bomb site in Addison Road. I wondered why Elena kept this rather grisly little item. Was it just because the body had been found up the road? Well, we'd never know now.

This time I actually lugged all the plastic sacks down three flights and outside. Tomorrow morning the dustmen would feed them into their grinder and that would be that. It was raining now, that fine sleet that drenches everything. The front garden looked dismal, the combination of dead, unpruned plants and unswept path made the place look like something we'd be well rid of. Suddenly I was really looking forward to being through with the whole thing. Katie had padded up the kitchen stairs and stood behind me.

'Let's see,' she said. My hand instinctively drew the cards back; I felt possessive and wanted to take them back to my lair to pore over in peace. But Katie took them and deciphered the tiny, regular words. 'They could be from anyone, that signature's just a squiggle.'

'I know, but they do seem to add up to someone reminding your father he was still around somewhere.'

'I agree with Chrissie, by rights he'd have forfeited his rights to the property, being a traitor and all. What's that bit of newspaper, can I look?'

'Something your mother saved about the Addison Road body.'

'Oh, that dreadful murder!' Katie fluttered. 'Did I tell you I was here when they found the body? I remember all the fuss, police cars, so noisy, the pavement all cordoned off. I wanted to go up there and offer to scan the bones for emanations because sensitives can often discern details that conventional methods miss, but Mother said we mustn't get involved and it was nothing to do with us. Someone came from the police, but Mother wasn't up to seeing them, it wasn't long before she passed on.'

'What did they want that time?'

'Well, of course, at the time they didn't realise there'd been foul play.'

'I suppose they were just talking to anyone who'd been round here before those houses were built, when there was still a bomb site,' I said.

'Ugh,' Katie grimaced. 'I wouldn't want to live in one of those houses, they must be impregnated with fear and sorrow, I don't know how it could ever be exorcised.'

CHAPTER THIRTEEN

When Marguerite came back to London in May she moved into the Ritz. Mr Paxton told me it looked as though the Kittermaster estate would have to meet at least some of her expenses and quoted Marguerite telling him she expected nothing but the best. She made herself memorable. Months later those who had served or supplied Marguerite were still talking about her. And later on I was to see the invoices, a stack of them that had been forwarded to Wootton Hardman. She doesn't seem to have paid for anything in cash so the items detailed made it only too easy to visualise the pattern of her days.

*   *   *

A handsome young waiter delivers a late breakfast on a long, narrow trolley covered with gleaming silver, porcelain and glass laid on a pink linen cloth. The napkin, in the same fabric, is so stiffly starched that it slides off the towelling robe, property of the hotel, in which Marguerite has wrapped herself after the masseur finished. Her skin smells pleasantly of soothing oils. She looks appreciatively at the beads of condensation on the ice-bucket which contains the jar of gleaming caviare. There are

136

little glass bowls of chopped onion and crumbled egg. She pours and sips pink champagne. The fruit bowl contains figs, the bloom on their purple skin making them almost grey, and velvety peaches. The toast is crisp and golden, the *pain au chocolat* crumbly and rich, the butter in curls as fine as wood shavings. Coffee is keeping warm in a silver vacuum jug. An elaborate arrangement of carnations and irises is on one side table, a tray of sherry and gin on the other and the mini-fridge is stacked with white wine, vodka and exotic mixers. A pile of new hard-backed novels she's treated herself to in Hatchards lies on the coffee table beside the latest glossy magazines. The concierge has guaranteed her tickets for tonight's performance of the hottest new show.

She rings the bell and when the waiter comes, orders more coffee just for the pleasure of being able to.

She picks up and glances through the letter she has already drafted on plain white paper. Without signing it, she slides it into one of the envelopes that did not have a monogram stamped on the flap. The stationery gave nothing except good quality away.

'Post this, will you?'

'Certainly, madam.'

Showered, made-up, dressed in the Armani trouser suit (grey pin-stripes, with a white shirt) she bought the previous day, Marguerite sets out to trawl the shops of Bond Street. She fancies a Chanel suit, dogtooth checks or pale pink tweed, complete with piping, gold buttons and weights in the hem to ensure a perfect hang. Pashmina shawls are big this season and Marguerite must have the superior variety, not cheapened and thickened with silk but a pure fine goats' hair shartoosh that will pass through her platinum wedding ring. She wants shoes and gloves and bags, some Mary Chess room fragrance and a few subtle velvet cushions from Georgina von Etzdorff to personalise her hotel suite, a brooch or pin to make a statement on her lapel.

By late afternoon numerous deliveries for Mrs Lang have been made to the Ritz. She has had her hair done at Michaeljohn. She is wearing a heavy antique chain from Wartski's, gold threaded with amethysts, and a jade green pashmina is loosely looped round her neck. She has taken afternoon tea with clotted cream scones and sponge cake in Brown's hotel and from there goes in a taxi the short distance to Arlington Street, telling the concierge to pay the driver and ordering a limo for the following day.

Marguerite strolls into the Ritz, breathes in its expensive melange of smells, turns towards the low tables where glamorous people sit drinking enticing cocktails, and sits down to order herself a Manhattan. Marguerite listens to Babel-babble as she downs the drink. 'Are there no natives left in London any more?' she says aloud. Then she gets up and walks through the lounge and hallway. She does not notice me behind her.

Deciding I wanted to talk to Marguerite about her late husband, I had been disappointed when the concierge, ringing up to her room, received no answer. 'She has come into the hotel, madam, you might find her in the bar,' he said, rightly. I might as well have been invisible. I followed her towards the lifts through a throng of celebratory, spangly people all pressing towards the private Marie Antoinette room to the right of a wide corridor. A chorus of guttural sibilants was interrupted by occasional English. The major-domo was announcing names—Mr and Mrs Goldman, Dr Sachs, Professor Hildesheim—interspersing them with the words, 'For Jonathan's bar mitzvah.'

Marguerite turned, bumping into an old man in a skull cap who said, *'Rev tov, ata medaber livrit.'*

'Sorry I don't understand,' Marguerite said, shaking her head, and to the lift operator, 'Is this place always so full of foreigners?'

'Marguerite!' I'd gone up in the neighbouring lift. 'May I come in and have a word?' I followed her into the suite's sitting-room, where her day's loot had already been delivered, a row of chic packages and bags carrying world-famous labels.

139

'Drink?' she offers.

'Oh, thanks so much, might I have something soft?'

'How did I guess?' she sighed. I saw her eyeing my clothes (a navy blue suit from Country Casuals) and my home-cut hair. She poured herself some gin and said discouragingly, 'I'm going out soon.'

'That's all right, I shan't keep you,' I promised. 'I just wondered if we could—that is, I thought we might have a little talk.' Marguerite stared at me without replying, big, exhausted blue eyes in a tanned face. I ploughed on. 'Now that I've realised that I do remember Justin, I'd so like to know what happened to him.'

'Why?'

'He had a great influence on my life. I'd love to know more about where you lived and what you both did.'

'No use asking me.' Marguerite drains her gin and pours another. 'We didn't keep in touch, me and Justin Lang.'

'But—'

'But he was my husband, but I'm his heir, but but but—that's another matter. It doesn't mean we lived together. We didn't even live in the same country. A great one for dropping out and hanging loose, my late husband was.'

'You said you've come from South Africa . . .'

'Trying to catch me out, are you?'

I wasn't, not that time at any rate, and said

140

quickly, 'No, really, it isn't that.' Then, because it was true, if perhaps a little disloyal, I added, 'As a matter of fact it doesn't make the slightest difference to me if it's you or the girls that inherit the estate, my job's just to make sure it's properly distributed and everything's done the right way, as the executor, you understand.'

'You always were ultra-conscientious,' Marguerite drawls.

'Why d'you say that?'

'It shows.'

Did it? Does it? I said, 'I suppose Aunt Elena had to find someone who was methodical and reliable.'

'Unlike her own daughters,' Marguerite murmured.

'The girls are more volatile than me, that's quite true. And of course they don't remember Justin, but I'm really interested in what happened to him. You say he wasn't in South Africa with you?'

'We'd been apart for a long time, by the time I settled there, Justin was a fly-by-night kind of guy, he scarpered off sharpish and left me holding the baby, but look, don't get this wrong, we didn't need to be Darby and Joan for me to inherit his share.'

'No, of course not,' I said.

Champagne, a Manhattan, and gin had loosened Marguerite's tongue. She said, 'He had a trick of disappearing.'

141

'Disappearing?' I prompted.

'He kept changing his name and changing his life, emigrated like he did from here in the first place—'

'Did he emigrate? Where did he settle?'

'Went to Israel, where else would he go, they were letting in anyone that said they were Jewish, the law of return it was called.'

The servant came in with two more packages and some fresh ice. I asked if I might use the bathroom, peeing quickly in a room full of expensive unguents and ointments, glancing into the extravagant bedroom where expensive clothes and luxurious knick-knacks lay on every flat surface. She's been spending a fortune here, I realised.

Unnoticed, I watched the chamber-man as he neatly plumped cushions and drew the curtains. 'It was you on duty this morning, right?' Marguerite said.

'Yes, madam.'

'What's your name?'

'Rick, madam.' He was an Aussie, tall and burly.

'Hi, Rick. You been here long? D'you have fun?' She emphasised the last word.

He looked at her cautiously. 'It can be interesting.'

'So did you have a good day?'

'Yes, thank you, madam.'

Marguerite took the swig that was one too many. She started to get up but fell back into her chair. 'Sho—so did I till this dried-up prude turned up.'

'I beg your pardon?'

'Mrs Merton, indeed! Married she may be, but frigid, I can tell.'

I felt myself flushing scarlet and sweat popping out on my face and neck. I took a few deep breaths, crossed my arms across my heaving chest. Keep calm, she isn't worth it.

'When did you ever let yourshelf—yourself—go?' Marguerite Lang, seeing me in the doorway, jeered.

'Now, this minute,' I responded, recovering the power of speech, and using it with unaccustomed vigour. 'You're offensive, you're disgustingly extravagant, you're greedy and grasping and wrong.'

'Over-privileged spoilt bitches, the lot of you.'

The waiter was opening the door. He looked very embarrassed. I gathered my tattered dignity around me and paused before leaving to say what was in my mind. 'One thing I do know. I'll see you damned before I let you get your filthy hands on any more of the Kittermasters' money.'

CHAPTER FOURTEEN

I felt—what's the word? Furious, yes, but also free/elated/volatile/released? I'd enjoyed letting myself go. I unloaded the story on Fidelis later that day and she told me it reminded her of the Tichbourne case. We'd been to a lecture in Burgh House—a fundraiser for a children's charity run by Israelis for the benefit of Palestinians in the Gaza strip. Though the slides had hardly made the place seem appealing, walking down the hill we discussed the possibility of going to Israel together. She said she wanted to see Jerusalem and experience for herself the vibes that had affected so many generations of travellers. I told her about the Negev observatory. Then I described the stars which, if it wasn't for the light-pollution, we'd have been able to see in Hampstead High Street on a clear night like this, the planets, Venus, brilliant and gibbous in the west, lying below right of the Pleiades this week, and Mars, brighter than every star but Sirius, Auriga and Capella above Taurus, Leo and Regulus high in the south-west, Arcturus in Bootesis in the east.

'You make it sound glorious. Maybe I'll come to your observatory too. Let's do it.'

'I'd love to, if only I ever get free of the

Lang problem.'

So she asked what I meant and responded with the words, 'The Tichbourne claimant.'

The name did ring a bell in my mind. 'Something about a long-lost heir?'

'Nobody was ever sure if the man who turned up to claim the title and estate was really the son who'd disappeared years before or just someone pretending to be him.'

'Oh God,' I groaned. 'She's a horrible woman, she's spending money that might not be hers like water, and the things she says—well, let's just say I don't like her. But your idea could let me in for an awful lot of trouble.' We walked side by side. Fidelis was softly humming the Leonore theme from *Fidelio*. I automatically ensured that my eyes didn't meet a stranger's, or my feet the little heaps of dog dirt which dot Hampstead's pavements. After a while I said, 'I could pretend you never gave me that idea.'

'Why?'

'Because if there's any chance it's true I'd have a duty to make sure, I'm the executor.'

'Would it matter so much? What's really at stake here?'

'Apart from the fact that she's—what shall I say?' Four-letter words suggested themselves, but I said, 'A cow,' and stopped by the window of the delicatessen. 'Let's get some food, come and have supper with me.'

'Love to. Something smells wonderful, I'm

hungry already, but just tell me first.'

I gazed absent-mindedly at the bowls of marinating meat and stuffed fish fillets and fresh pasta in subtle sauces and spicy, elaborate salads. 'What's at stake?' I counted the items off on my fingers. 'There's the value of the house minus forty per cent tax. It's pretty run down, but a similar one sold for eight million pounds. Even if you divide by half that leaves a small fortune for the girls, they'd neither of them ever need to work again. But that's not all. Bertram may not have lived like a rich man but he turns out to have been rolling in cash.'

'The Nobel prize is big money.'

'Yes, but he had far more than that could have accounted for, and if it was what he inherited from Pearl, then everything becomes really complicated. There was a collection of ivory and jade. I'd completely forgotten it till that woman reminded me, it lived in a red lacquer cabinet covered with funny little people in conical hats, and trees and bridges—willow pattern stuff, you know what I mean?'

'Good chinoiserie can be very valuable, I believe.'

'This lot was, I'd say priceless if that wasn't a contradiction in terms. The ivories were sent for sale in Geneva and you just wouldn't believe how much it fetched, and the jade made a bomb at Sotheby's in the eighties, right at the top of the boom. But Marguerite said all the Chinese stuff had been Pearl Lang's too. The total's huge, it means there's literally millions at stake. A fortune.'

We spent an amount that, in any other context, would have seemed extravagant, on chunks of hot-smoked salmon, artichoke and avocado salad, walnut bread, and fresh figs. Then Fidelis stopped off in her own flat to pick up some wine. When she came in carrying a bottle of 1993 Meursault, I remarked on the quiet. 'Our neighbours must have gone out, what a blessed relief.'

'They are all at the hospital, Bill had a bike crash.'

'Bill?'

'He's the youngest boy, the one who wants to do psychology at college.'

'I don't think I know any of their names, to me they are just an undifferentiated gang.'

'Oh, no, Vicky, there's Ben, he works at the zoo, and Ken's a life saver at the Highgate Ponds and poor Bill, he's been trying to make some money despatch riding.' She gave me a quizzical look and said, 'Their bark's worse than their bite.' Embarrassed to admit that I'd been afraid of both bite and bark, I went and made some unnecessary adjustments to the salad. Fidelis poured wine and tactfully turned the subject back to the long-lost heir.

Over the dregs she said, 'You might need an inquiry agent.'

'I suppose Paxton might recommend

147

someone.'

'Or you could always go and see for yourself.'

'Where? What?' I realised that my voice was a tiny bit slurred; I'm not used to alcohol, for I never drink on my own at all, and very little when I go out, on account of driving. I don't like the sensation of relaxed control, when my cheeks are hot and my lips feel loose and my words don't come out quite as crisply as I expect.

'You could go to South Africa and make some inquiries about Marguerite Lang. At the estate's expense—you'd cost less than a private detective.'

The star map for the southern hemisphere flashed through my mind. 'I'd really love to,' I said. 'But I don't think I can. For various reasons.'

'Come now, Victoria.' Suddenly Fidelis sounded more motherly than my own mother ever had.

'Fidelis, really, can you see me making intimate inquiries?'

'What are you, Victoria, a character out of Anita Brookner?'

I was even wearing a cardigan that evening, a long grey one with pockets. Thrusting my hands into them, just like a Brookner heroine, I said, 'Is that so dreadful?'

'Limiting, perhaps. But people can change,' Fidelis said, in an implicit reminder that she's

148

a psychiatrist.

'You mean lose my inhibitions?'

She said, 'Be what you wish to seem. Seem what you wish to be.'

'Who said that?'

'I can never remember, nor can I make out which is the right way round. All the same, either way it's a good thought, wouldn't you say?'

'Maybe, but I still couldn't.'

'I think you could. Begin by taking yourself off to ask some questions. Enjoy the sun. Look at the Southern Cross. Have an affair.'

'Oh, nobody ever makes passes at me,' I told her.

'You aren't sending out the right signals.'

'That's what Stuart used to tell me.'

'And would you like people to make passes at you?' Psychiatrists ask questions, their patients give truthful answers. It is not what my favourite author describes as a civilised mode of conversation.

'I'd still like to think Mr Right's out there somewhere,' I said, an admission I had never made to anyone else. And then I pulled myself together. This wasn't a consulting room, Fidelis was my neighbour, not my shrink. So I said:

'What about you?' I saw faint surprise on her face. Fidelis wasn't used to being asked questions in her turn. She must be in her mid-sixties, looks her age but elegant with it. Yes, she has wrinkles; but her nose is narrow, her skin olive, her dark eyebrows sharply marked under a swing of well-cut silver hair.

'I?' she asked. 'Oh, that's all old history now.'

So Fidelis has a history. She was probably never repressed or restrained, unlike me. There's something to be said for having no family to live up to. As an adult, she'd have been free, unattached, answerable to nobody. Without the weight of the collective Kittermaster gaze I might have been a quite different woman. A woman who broke her contracts to jaunt off to a different hemisphere at the drop of a hat. 'I can't go,' I said. 'I've got a deadline.'

'Can't it be put off?'

'Not if I ever want another commission.'

CHAPTER FIFTEEN

The first batch of Elena's journal, transcribed, translated and typed out, arrived with apologies from the post-grad student I'd employed to do the work. She'd found the spidery little writing hard to decipher; she was having trouble with her thesis. I'd told her, hadn't I, that it wasn't urgent. Excuses, excuses.

The first entry was dated New Year's Eve 1957. Elena had been in England for just over a year, having (as I knew) arrived as a refugee after the October 1956 uprising. I could hear her voice now, telling me she'd never been 'a political' herself, but she was obviously going to grab the chance of getting out to the West when she saw it. As she said, 'Who wouldn't?'

I knew she'd got a job waitressing in a club in St James's. It was Bertram's club, so perhaps he'd got her the job. Certainly they got married within a few months of her arrival.

She began her diary with a list of good resolutions, ranging from the moral—*Remember how fortunate I am*—through the practical—*Get up earlier in the morning*—to the aspirational—*Read Proust.*

I skimmed through the pages of typescript. They should have been objectively fascinating, a description of England from a stranger's candid viewpoint, but consisted largely of matter-of-fact details of what she'd cooked, which conformed to the old pattern, perhaps required by her husband, of roast on Sunday, cold on Monday, hash on Tuesday, shepherd's pie on Wednesday and the last pitiful remains of the Sunday joint turned into a concoction laughingly called curry, before Friday's fish. On Saturday she occasionally ran to a goulash.

That first year she was often sick, being pregnant. At Easter she wrote, *Sheila plus Victoria to tea, eggs in garden.* But she wrote on irregular days, one couldn't have reconstructed a timetable, and in this first batch there was no mention of Justin Lang.

151

CHAPTER SIXTEEN

Hilly's base was a room in Ealing that the estate agent called a studio flat. Her mother said it was just a bed-sitter by another name, insanitary and ludicrously over-priced, and she didn't understand why Hilly couldn't just commute from her real home, in Gerrard's Cross. Hilly always insisted she needed to be near her work and friends, but what she really meant was that she had to have a place of her own because even if she didn't actually like living in a tip, she needed the freedom to prove she could. And a tip it was. She hung her clothes from pegs on the wall or stacked them in wire baskets on the floor. She washed up in her cupboard-kitchen when there was nothing left to use. The only thing she kept clean was the bath. Clothes sorting took place only when she was packing for a trip.

Due to escort a party of art enthusiasts to the Northern Capitals, Hilly decided she'd require something formal and warm, so found her one black suit, brushed off the plaster dust and mould that bubbled from the walls, and wondered where she'd left her black bag. Not under the bed, not in a wire rack; eventually she found it on a hook behind the flannel shirt and guernsey.

It was a better bag than she'd ever have

bought herself. She'd had a day conducting the partners of American bankers (the bankers were all male, the partners all female) round London's more expensive department stores. On their last stop, in Liberty's, the boss-wife had produced, with a flourish, a bag Hilly had been seen fingering. Her thanks had been profuse. While she uttered them, Hilly wondered how to ask for the receipt so as to trade the lavish gift in for cash the next day—a lot of cash, as much as she earned in a week. But she couldn't think of a polite way to say it, so used the bag for best instead, a capacious, heavy container full of compartments and pockets. She turned it upside down over the bed. A selection of the usual detritus fell out of its crevices. Safety pins, a tampon, coins, boiled sweets gone soggy in their cellophane, the long-lost key to the bag's own lock, and an unlabelled floppy disk.

Hilly's employers went in for high-tech methods. They expected their tour guides and couriers to have computers and would not have approved if they'd known Hilly always printed everything out on to paper and carried old-fashioned clipboards and folders round the world. Now she booted up to check whether this one, which must have fallen into her open bag, referred to a past or future trip.

There was only one file listed and she didn't know the name so brought it up to check on screen.

What was this?

1956–1960, Arab espionage plots against Israel followed by a list of names. *Shin Bet, Palmach, Unit 131. Places: Jerusalem, Dirnona. G.D.K. McCormick,* The Israeli Secret Service *197 identifies the following: Colonel Da, Max Bennett; tortured to death in a Cairo prison, 1955, Elie Cohen.*

Another heading. *Projects run in Egypt in the early 1960s by German scientists with some American involvement. Ibis, a plan to inject missiles with cobalt 60 and strontium 90 atomic waste. Cleopatra, an atomic weapon. Osiris, means of delivering bacteriological weapons.*

That meant germ warfare. Hilly remembered with hideous, regrettable clarity what had been said on the subject in Manchuria. Surely, she thought, after Eichmann and Ishii, nobody could have continued planning such crimes? Hilly was a child of peace-time. Hilly's mum always said 'Things are for the best in the best of all possible worlds.' Shuddering, Hilly wanted to shut corrupting contradiction from her mind.

What was all this, anyway? Hilly realised that the disk must be Ari's, and remembered him dropping things on the floor when they took a taxi away from Golders Green. This was the disk she'd picked up and failed to run after him with. She hadn't used the bag since, and semi-purposefully (because she was ashamed) had let the disk go out of her mind.

She scrolled on down.

Isser Harel writes 'Ibis, Cleopatra and Isis were projects with the intention of destroying Israel.' Then she came upon a quotation from the Cairo newspaper *Al-Ahram*. *'The Israelites had a perfect system of intelligence in Egypt.'*

Looks as though they needed it, Hilly said aloud, and thought, Is this what Ari's work's about? Was he working on more recent history, rather than concentrating on research into wartime atrocities? Later such threats had been averted—must have been, she thought, for she'd had no idea anyone even contemplated the use of such weapons after the Second World War was over. But human malevolence is inextinguishable. Wasn't there something about Iraq and the Kurds? Images of child victims floated back into her unwelcoming mind. Had that been germ warfare? Or maybe poison gas. It didn't bear thinking about. But Ari seemed to be thinking about it all the time.

I wonder if Ari's a spy, she thought suddenly. His country still has enemies, maybe there's still plans to—to do *that* to them. Maybe the threat never went away.

It made her want to find Ari and grab hold of him, hold him in her own tight, warm embrace and keep him safe. One woman against the world.

CHAPTER SEVENTEEN

B comes back from a lecture telling me he has invited J to lunch on Saturday. That is the morning I always go to the Continental delicatessen in Notting Hill, and when I get back Mrs B is in the nursery with the girls and J is in the kitchen telling Mrs Beak's granddaughter about astronomy, which is his hobby. She is a sulky, hostile girl. I suspect her of stealing money from my bag and food from the larder when she has a chance. It is a tax I pay, these Saturdays, to keep Mrs Beck sweet for the rest of the week. She values coming to a house with so famous an employer. When B went to see the Prime Minister she must have boasted about it all over West London. How else would the information have reached the Evening Standard? B was unconcerned, having grown up with servants and well aware what to expect. He says they always know more about our affairs than we do and it's just one of those things. But he always keeps his study door locked.

J is much as usual, which is to say neither grateful nor gracious. If that is what years at an English public school do for the young—well, my Katarina and Christina shall stay at home with me. Perhaps it is fortunate after all that I have no son, since B would insist on sending him away at the age of seven as is usual for boys of his class—

monstrous!

J doesn't stop talking to Marlene when I come in, nor does she rise to her feet. She looks at him as though he were a film star, she has a crush on him. While I am preparing the lunch, J starts telling the girl about politics. I think he is doing it to annoy me. He puts silly, unsuitable notions into her head, talking about redistributing wealth and creating equality. I tell them sharply that I have seen only too much of a society in which such ideas have been put into practice, and I want to hear no more of it here. I see them grin at each other in a kind of complicity which offends me. I am not easy in J's company, since I feel he is at once suspicious and mocking, and I look always for traces of HER in him.

After lunch B and J shut themselves up in the study. Do they speak of her? I can understand nothing. From the passage outside I hear that they are talking about B's work. Infection, dissemination, protection, cross-contamination. It is his work that B talks about to this boy, work he would never discuss with me. Experiments, they describe, results, subjects. They get excited about it, B's voice is agitated, emotional as otherwise I only hear him at night, in bed. This work that takes him to America and out of London to the country, Dorset, Cornwall—I begin to hate it. I wouldn't understand, oh no, not Elena, all I'm good for is looking after the house and the children. And making love.

157

CHAPTER EIGHTEEN

Gayle's secretary had forwarded on to me some of the sections 'her writer' had roughed out before his contract was rewritten. Gayle presumably thought these details were harmless and acceptable as far as they went, which was boringly far, unabbreviated information about minute sociological and genealogical facts readable—if at all—only by a member of the family or by a social historian. This would certainly not have made what publishers call a 'commercial' book.

I'd known, though vaguely, of most of these characters. There was the copper miner from Gloucestershire who established the family fortune, his preacher son and the one who went to open a mine on Dartmoor, the eldest of the next generation whose wife brought Portheglos into the family, the ever widening family tree with its generations of scholars, politicians, reformers and writers; the do-gooding wives and daughters, the benevolent educationalists, the ambitious cousins, the increasingly grand families into which they married. The First World War, the Great Depression.

Either this was the point at which the writer had been called off or this was as much as Gayle was willing to let me read. What she'd forgotten was that Marcus Foster had been to see others in the family. He had left me his number. I didn't tell Gayle, though it made me feel oddly guilty, as though I was still the wet little girl who was dominated by big bossy cousin Gayle.

In the train down to Cambridge to meet Marcus Foster I let my imagination roam. What could have provoked Gayle's censorious (secretive? censoring?) shock-horror? Had there been a thief in the family? Or a murderer? Had one of the now distinguished oldies once been drunk in charge of a car or riotous in front of a policeman? Or—and this seemed more plausible—Marcus Foster might have found proof that Bertram really had been 'a Cambridge spy', the fifth or sixth or seventh man, another traitor from Trinity.

I was a student in Cambridge (now not called undergraduates any more, Luke says, because the word creates class barriers) but I have so seldom been back that I'd forgotten my way round. I decided to walk from the station to Trinity College and was appalled to realise how far it was, plod plod along a road I must always have whizzed down on a bike. Or laboured down, for I know my memories of undergraduate life are rather glorified, having edited out the parties I was not invited to, the evenings I was alone in my room, the men who didn't give me a second glance, the sexual adventures I never had. I'd also forgotten how

159

cold it could be even in summer; pretty, brilliantly coloured and flowery, but the spiteful wind off the fens attacked my reddening cheeks and watering eyes. I looked at buildings and couldn't recall if they had always been there. And had the traffic always been so relentless?

My feet hurt. I had silly shoes on, owing to some unformed and idiotic hope of impressing Marcus Foster. Now, of course, I can't believe I cared, can't remember the thought process at all, but I must have, or I wouldn't have put on the hound's-tooth check Chanel suit Gayle once passed on to me and the high-heeled shoes that pressed on my big toes. Pointless. Silly. A humiliating memory—for Marcus Foster was not only half my age but also self-evidently gay.

At first I was surprised that Gayle had not forbidden him to speak to me but then I made a pretty good guess at her reasons. Doing so would have made him realise there was something worth concealing in the material he'd collected and then he might try selling it to someone who would pay even more to hear it than she, by commissioning an alternative book, was paying.

Marcus evidently hadn't given the matter much thought. The only thing he was really interested in was his novel, a frank, no-holds-barred exposé of a middle-class youth. He began to tell me about the miseries of life as the brother of an anorexic supermodel. Even I had heard of Emily Foster. They might have seemed the perfect family, he said, absent-minded architect father, committee-attending, bridge—and tennis-playing mother, two point four children—an anthropomorphised spaniel counting as the point four—nice suburban house and garden, but you wait, he warned, just wait till I've taken the lid off that cosy little idyll.

All this was so absorbing to him that the implications of his pot-boiling research into the Kittermasters had evidently passed Marcus Foster by. He didn't hesitate to tell me he had some information about Bertram Kittermaster, he doubted there was anything until after the war. I interjected with a question about the newspaper slanders concerning spying, and he said no, he'd found no sign of anything as interesting as that, nobody'd taken that idea very seriously had they, but he'd print out a set of the relevant notes for me. I watched him call the file called Kittermaster on to his screen and set 'find' to the word Bertram.

As the pages reeled slowly off the printer, I waited in his little room, wondering whether its bleak tidiness was due to poverty or temperament. It didn't look much like the student digs I remembered.

Marcus clipped the document together for me and had obviously forgotten my existence

161

before I was well out of the door. I had a nostalgic, voyeuristic snack in the overcrowded Copper Kettle and took a taxi back to the station.

I hadn't taken any notice of the man on the platform, though he'd walked towards me as the train came in and we got into the same second-class coach. He smiled, I smiled. He was the kind of person I might well know, a professorial type on his way to some pompous dinner in London, I assumed, as Stuart used to and Stuart's colleagues still did, commuting for evening functions from Oxford or Cambridge, establishment types in dinner jackets whom nobody would ever take for waiters. This one looked seventy-odd with cheery pink cheeks, hooded blue eyes and an air of responsibility and tolerance. A lawyer? A doctor? No. He was an anthropologist and a cousin. 'You're Victoria, aren't you? Haven't seen you since— oh, ages ago, one time at Portheglos. How's your boy?'

Embarrassingly I had no idea who this was. I swivelled my eyes towards his battered leather briefcase and saw the initials were J. J. K. Saying, 'Luke's fine, thanks,' I thought, John? James? Jeremy?

'And Stephen?'

'Stuart. Fine too, as far as I know, but we're divorced.' He sat opposite me and pulled from his case a copy of the *Argus* and some papers in a transparent plastic folder. 'Excuse me, can

162

I just . . .' In reaching to pull the curtain unnecessarily forward across our reflected faces, I was able to push the newspaper aside and expose the top document in his folder which, luckily, was a letter. I read what I needed upside down. Dear Jeff. Jeffrey Kittermaster, of course, my second or third cousin, an ethnographer, expert on nomadic peoples.

We exchanged some more pleasantries. I dredged up a memory, fortunately accurate, of his dentist wife and doctor daughter. We agreed we both had some work to do and began to read as the train trotted through the dark countryside.

Marcus Foster's degree was in history so he'd done the usual research, libraries, conversations, trips to the Public Record Office. Some material was still classified in Britain, not released for public scrutiny under the thirty year rule, but lots of it was available in America too, so he'd invoked the Freedom of Information Act and received copies of documents that were still secret here. The first mention of Bertram's name that his notes included came in 1903, when he was born, only son of David and Bernadette Kittermaster. Then we jump to the late 1940s. Bertram is already a well-known scientist based at the research centre at Porton Down.

It was obvious that Marcus Foster didn't understand the science any more than I do, or the ambience and emotions of the Cold War period. But he knew Bertram had been working on bacterial defences against bacterial attack. In other words, of course—and we'd better be realistic about it—he'd been developing weapons, for you can't make an effective shield unless you know how the enemy's sword gets used. In fact to make a shield you need to have a sword.

Is that a sufficient justification for the infamous trade our family's great man had been following? I really didn't know and still don't. In those days people must have feared the Russians would use such weapons, and if not the Russians, the Chinese or—but I realised, as my thoughts reached this point, that I wasn't well enough informed about modern history to guess what other states might have been seen as dangerous. In the forties the Korean War was going on. The Hungarian crisis was in 1956, I knew that because it was the year Elena got to England. Or what about Suez, which was in the same year? Did they fear that Egypt might have such weapons?

But the Cold War had dominated the period, as well as the following decades. And with a sudden shock of dismay I wondered if Bertram really had been one of the Cambridge spies after all.

'Are you all right, Victoria, you've gone quite pale, shall I get you a cup of tea?'

I quickly discounted any fleeting idea that Bertram could have misused his expertise, an unlikely notion if ever there was one, and said, 'No, no, thanks, I'm fine, I was just surprised.'

'What are you working on at the moment?'

An academic's first question. I replied, 'I've been diverted from philology for the moment by winding up Bertram and Elena's estate.'

'Oh, I do sympathise, that's always a much more tiresome chore than one expects,' he said. 'My father-in-law's took a year out of my life. Are you sole executor?'

'For my sins.'

'Having trouble with the family, are you? Legacies can poison relationships in my experience. Aren't there some children?'

'Katie and Christina.'

'Oh yes, nice girls—not that I've seen them to speak to for years, we used to meet down at Portheglos but I don't seem to get there so much these days. What happened to them, those two girls?'

'Christina's just come back from some years in the States, she's a nurse and has a couple of children.'

'Another in the tradition of strong-minded Kittermaster women?'

'Both of them are. Katie's a newspaper columnist.'

He looked impressed. 'Really, is she? What's she write about?'

'I'm afraid she calls herself an astrologer.'

'What—predictions and prophecies?'

I saw that there was a copy of Katie's paper on a table across the aisle, asked the man who wasn't reading it whether I could and unfolded it to show Jeff, asking, 'D'you know your birth sign?'

'No idea. My birthday's early September.'

'That means you're Virgo, like me—you couldn't have spent months with Katie and not know. Listen. *The sun is in Libra, the moon is in Capricorn and Mars goes into Cancer, so you are lucky. Love, games, exotic travel, adventures, now's the time to get out of your old rut and break rules. Your future is out there, waiting for you, follow your own star and find your own ideal.* There you are, Jeff, what's your ideal?'

'God knows. And yours?'

'Ditto,' I said, lying. My ideal was too embarrassing to utter to anyone else and almost too improbable to admit to myself. Catching my thought, Jeff said:

'It's all aimed at lovesick kids, not old buffers. By my time of life one settles for a good night's sleep.'

'Well, I wouldn't say no to that either,' I agreed. 'Actually, Jeff, you might be able to help with something. D'you happen to remember Bertram when you were young?'

'The great man, yes, of course, we used to see something of him at home and then he was very kind when I came out of the army— National Service, you know, we all had to do it

166

in those days. I'd gone into the army at seventeen, stationed in Kenya, and Bertram helped get me into Cambridge when I was demobbed in 1949.'

'I should have got in touch with you before.' I told him about Marguerite Lang. And— bingo. He said:

'I don't think I ever knew Pearl, she was caught in the blitz when I'd have been quite young, but of course I knew Justin.'

'You knew Justin!'

'Daresay I'm about the last person still around who did.'

'You're certainly the first I've found.' I was interrupted by the announcement that we were approaching King's Cross. 'Jeff, have you got time to talk? It would really help if—'

But he was in a hurry, already late for a dinner at Lancaster House. As he dashed ahead of me through the rush hour crowd, grey curls and brown gabardine coat tails flying, to plunge into the Underground, he called back, 'Tomorrow at the Reform, eleven, OK?' but can hardly have heard my shouted agreement.

There was never any rhyme or reason to my insomnia and that night was a bad one. None of my tried and tested tricks for getting to sleep worked, though for once there wasn't even a rumpus coming through the party wall.

I went over mental lists of stars and galaxies, I imagined myself in a room with all surfaces covered in black velvet, I spent a lottery win, I relaxed each muscle in turn. I even allowed myself the thought I tried never to indulge (because if you give voice to your innermost desires, fate will ensure you never achieve them) and concocted a fantasy about a dark, powerful, clever man who'd start talking to me in a train, no, a library, a man who obviously liked me at first sight and then loved and lusted and—stop. Rather than indulging in impossible dreams, it would even be better to fret about tomorrow's petty rendezvous.

I must have nodded off a bit, though it didn't feel like it when I got up. But the day improved. When I went out there was one solitary boy in the street. He had a bandage over one eye and didn't take any notice of me but I made myself say, 'Hullo, Bill, how are you feeling?' and he replied with perfect civility that he was OK. A good sign, which was followed by the Northern line not being on strike or go slow. Jeff was waiting for me when I arrived at his club in Pall Mall and took me to sit on leather chairs at a table in a galleried hall which was faced and floored with elaborate multi-coloured stone mosaics. I suddenly recognised it as the clubland setting of—had it been the televised John le Carré novels, or Ian Fleming? Whether Smiley or Bond, I realised afterwards it had been some kind of omen of what Jeff was going to tell me about Justin Lang.

'He was an attractive chap. Good-looking, clever, charming. I don't think I knew him when we were kids though we were much the same age. I knew him well before the trouble.'

'The trouble?' I prompted.

'Yes, well, it's never spoken of.'

'What was it?'

'I doubt there are many people left to remember it now. All hushed up at the time, of course, it wouldn't have done old Bertram any good if it got out and it's not as though they were actually related. Come to think, though, I suppose it's why the old man's name's turning up in tabloids now he's dead.'

'Jeff—' I began.

'You haven't told me why you're interested,' he said. 'Not writing a book, are you?'

As I explained Jeff listened with a non-committal, assessing expression on his face, as though I were a research student presenting a dubious thesis. 'It would help a lot if I could understand more about all this, Jeff,' I pleaded.

'Yes, I can see that. Well, for your ears only . . .'

Jeff's first job after National Service and university was a lectureship at the University of London, and it was at that time that he happened to meet Justin Lang. 'Funnily enough I remember it well, I'd looked in to hear a lecture of Bertram's, didn't understand a word of course, but when a cousin turns up

169

at your college you feel duty-bound, so I sat through an hour of bacteria and cross-infection and then walked to the Tube with the old man. Not so old, come to think of it, this must have been the mid-fifties, he'd have been years younger than I am now. But at the time he seemed ancient and distinguished in a shabby sort of way, Elena can't have been around yet. So there we are, walking across the square and up comes this man, tall, dark, Jewish of course, Justin Lang. Bertram didn't say anything about being related to him but they were quite friendly. Bertram introduced us and we talked about climbing. Justin and Bertram had both done the Munros. I was a bit of a climber myself, so after that I went with Justin sometimes. Remarkable chap, he wasn't an astronomer, he'd done history at Manchester, but he knew the name of every single star and constellation in the sky.'

'What did he do?'

'Some kind of civil service job, nothing specially interesting.'

'But you knew he was Bertram's stepson?'

'I suppose so. I certainly did later on. Afterwards.'

'Did you ever see them together?'

'Not at family dos, Justin wasn't ever part of that. I did go round to Addison Road with Justin a couple of times, gloomy, chilly great barn of a place.'

'Did Justin ever say it belonged to him?'

'Certainly not, he was as much a guest there as I was, specially after Bertram married Elena. She'd issue formal invitations to luncheon on a Saturday.'

'I remember that. I sometimes went with my mother.'

'Well then, you might have seen Justin yourself.'

'I don't remember him there. He told me star names at Portheglos once though.'

'He should have been a teacher, had a knack of putting ideas into heads. What a waste it all was.'

'But Jeff, I'm back to the same question— how come Justin disappeared from view, why doesn't anyone remember him?'

Jeff said very few people ever knew of the relationship, though he did remember someone once making the mistake (corrected with equal speed by both Justin himself and Bertram) of thinking Justin's surname was Kittermaster. Which made it all the more embarrassing when things, as Jeff put it, went pear-shaped.

At this point Jeff asked me to excuse him— 'Too much coffee, it's a diuretic'—and went across the hall. When he came back, he sat down and said, 'I've been thinking, Victoria, you need to understand about the time we're talking about, before you were even born.'

'I was born in 1950.'

'Well, you won't really remember, it's even

hard for me to think myself back into the state of mind. The fifties were a peculiar decade in this country. People used to say we'd won the war but lost the peace. Things were pretty austere, you know, food rationing, smelly and dirty—you couldn't get enough paint or materials for doing things up. There were bomb craters in the streets. And we were all extraordinarily meek.'

'Weren't there Aldermaston marches?'

'Yes, for some people, but most of us didn't want to ban the bomb, we were simply—well, you could call it passive. As one of my contemporaries remarked recently, rebellion hadn't been invented yet. Maybe everyone was exhausted, after the war. Scared too. We lived in the shadow of the bomb. Looking back, I don't know how we dared to bring children into the world at all. It probably sounds over-dramatic to say one lived in dread but a lot of us really were genuinely afraid. That's the real generation gap, Victoria, because you lot aren't. Russia, China, communism, the gulags, the mushroom cloud—it was a different world from this.' He gestured round the self-confident ambience of his club. I suddenly remembered some gossip about Jeff, though from the appearance of this benign establishment-man you'd never guess that he'd suffered frequent episodes of depression so severe as to put him in a mental hospital. He said, 'It's been a bad century.'

'I don't remember things seeming so bad when I was little,' I said.

'You were too young to notice.'

'But I've read books, seen movies, looked at pictures—was it really so dismal?'

'I suppose the mass of people did carry on all oblivious, just trying to get back to real life after the disruption of the war. But then one was brought up short. When Justin left—that was a shock. Brought everything home, if you know what I mean.'

'Left?'

'Escaped. Ran away.'

'Look, Jeff, I'm lost. What d'you mean, escaped? What from?'

'Oh. What from. Well—the law, prosecution, thirty years in high security, that kind of thing.'

I looked closely at the benign old face. Could this all be an elaborate tease? 'What had he done?' I asked.

'Given secrets to the enemy, what d'you think?'

'Secrets? I thought you said he was a civil servant. What secrets did he have to tell?'

Jeff gestured at a passing waiter and ordered gin. 'I know it's a bit early but talking about Justin's getting me down. I missed him, you know, after he'd gone. There was something about the man.'

But Jeff had to overcome a long habit of silence about this matter; there followed another trip to the lavatory, two more gins, an exchange with a passing clubman about the best tour operator for Nile cruises, and some diversions through the early novels of Kingsley Amis and Anthony Powell before Jeff brought himself to tell me what Justin Lang had done.

Justin had stolen secret information from Bertram and passed it to 'the enemy'. He was never prosecuted because he'd escaped just in time, nobody knew where. The story had never got out because, while the research and stockpiling of nuclear weapons was well known to be taking place, nobody in authority had ever admitted that bacteriological weapons were being made or even developed. If Justin had been exposed as a thief and a spy, then the details of what he'd stolen would also have had to be revealed.

I said I didn't understand. How could Justin have got access to Bertram's work? It didn't sound, from what I'd heard so far, that they were on intimate terms. Surely Bertram wouldn't have taken Justin to Porton, to his lab?

Jeff returned to his earlier theme. 'Of course not, but you don't remember the fifties, Victoria, it's hard to imagine now. We didn't have computers, we didn't even have faxes or photocopiers.'

'We didn't in my time either, Jeff, I didn't even get my first electronic typewriter till the seventies.'

'Well, in the fifties we had paper and carbons and when we took work home, we took pages and files full of it. There's a Bratby sketch picture in the Moorsom, d'you know it, hordes of men walking to the Tube, all wearing bowlers or trilbies and carrying bulging briefcases. These days a year's results fit on to a three and a half inch floppy.' He took one out of an inner breast pocket, a little piece of red plastic, and added, 'That's my new book about the Brazilian Yanomami, all two hundred thousand words of it.'

'Are you saying that Justin stole Bertram's papers from Addison Road?'

'That's about the size of it.'

'So what happened then?'

'Well, I wouldn't know exactly, being young and not involved. Nobody did know actually, there'd have been a major scandal if it hadn't been hushed up, and I only got some idea of it because I was questioned about Justin.'

'By Bertram?'

'No, he never mentioned the matter again, not to me at any rate, he wasn't exactly chatty as you might recall, but the authorities got on Justin's trail.'

'Police?'

'I think they were some kind of spooks, but it didn't matter who they were because I couldn't help, I hadn't any notion what had happened to him. He'd just upped and left.'

'But Jeff, I can't understand how nobody

knew. Everyone I asked, all the family, none of them even remembered Justin.'

'Not many would ever have come across him and anyone who did know didn't want to talk about him, more likely.'

'This certainly explains why Uncle Edgar got so ratty, I suppose he's afraid of the story coming out.'

'It could still be embarrassing.'

I pressed him. 'Didn't you ever discover where Justin went? I mean, it's all such old history, he could have got in touch or sent some sort of message. You said you were friends.'

'There were sightings,' Jeff mumbled. It was his cue for retreating into rather unconvincing old bufferhood, and if I hadn't really cared I'd have let it go at that, but the idea of my Star Man held an inexplicable appeal and when he came back (again) from the lavatory, following him out of the club, across The Mall, up St James's Square and to the Tube at Green Park, I probed and pressed the old man.

He said he'd heard the chap was in New Guinea, fifteen, twenty years ago, someone had been on a cruise and spotted him in Port Moresby. 'But that's it, Victoria, I don't know any more than that and I shouldn't have told you as much.'

From the *Kensington and Chelsea Chronicle*, 24 May 1999

Bomb site skeleton named

Checks of missing person records dating back to 1950 have revealed the identity of the skeleton found during excavation of a swimming pool at the Addison Road home of media tycoon Jacques-Yves Chapelier, who bought the five-bedroomed home in 1997. Pathologists found the skeleton was that of a murdered man, not, as initially thought, of a victim of war-time bombs. Today Notting Hill police announced that the remains fit the description of Dr Tomo Matsuzakara, an American businessman who disappeared from his London hotel in February 1962. Police inquiries are continuing.

CHAPTER NINETEEN

I was fired with the thought of Justin Lang. Having remembered him, it came to me that it was he who had always been my pattern of an ideal man; in boys I'd gone out with at university, in my husband and my only lover I found imitation, dark, burly, deep-voiced men. Voices matter a lot to me. Justin's, hushed and impersonal, comes back to me, speaking of Cassiopeia.

I was also fired by burgeoning resentment against Marguerite Lang. It simply wasn't right for her to be splashing around all that money that still could prove not to be hers. As for her rudeness to me, it was probably unreasonable to hold it against her, given that she'd been drunk that day at the Ritz. No, it's not unreasonable to despise drunkards. She should be ashamed to lose control like that. The fact that I probably wouldn't have given a damn if she'd chosen a more implausible insult and called me a thief, maybe, or a slag, was neither here nor there. Her behaviour was beyond the pale. But she called me a prude. And frigid. On this private page, for you only to read, writing about what is past and over, I can admit that she hit home and hurt.

And I had 'the girls' on my back. We'd stopped clearing the house out because Mr

Paxton said selling it would have to be on hold till its ownership was sorted out, but Katie, with the attitude of a child hugging to her chest any toy someone else was trying to take away, had moved upstairs, sleeping in the only room left furnished on the sofa in her mother's boudoir and psychically prepared to repel boarders. She'd already agreed a sale of her own apartment in Norwich and nearly exchanged contracts on the rather grand cottage in Suffolk she was going to buy with her inheritance, but of course that was on hold too.

Both girls went on and on about the situation, and I went on making myself be patient with them. The tape on my answering machine ran out, I had a thickening pile of written arguments—you'd have thought the whole thing was my responsibility. Well, of course some of it was, but not all. I couldn't do anything about 'the shame Justin Lang had brought upon the family' which is a phrase both girls kept repeating after I told them what I'd learnt about him. Christina was damned if her family home was going to end up in the hands of a bloody traitor, or even his widow's hands. 'After all my father did for him', she said, which I thought was pretty rich considering that by all accounts all Bertram had done was neglect the child and ignore the man.

I'd really had enough, especially as I was

179

tense about my own work too. It was overdue but on temporary hold, waiting for a detailed critique from my American colleague, a brilliant lexicographer, who was away incommunicado on honeymoon—his fifth. Why couldn't I tell the girls I was too busy to go round these repetitive conversational loops, even if it wasn't true? Anyone else would have done and I wished I could but I suffer from invincible truthfulness. I can't make myself lie however hard I try. My truth will always out.

Then I had a sympathetic call from Mr Paxton who, like me, was treated to the girls' tirades. 'You sound at the end of your tether,' he remarked and I told him I'd been terribly busy, as well as having had flu.

'Oh yes, so did I, it was quite an epidemic this time, doesn't it get one down?'

We discussed checking up on Marguerite's story. It would be necessary to have third party evidence that she'd lived in South Africa, as she'd told us, and moved there from Israel, and that she was the wife of Justin Lang. The certificates were some kind of proof, of course, but it would take proper investigations in South Africa before Wootton Hardman could be satisfied.

'It must be lovely there,' I remarked, looking out of my window at parallel stripes of rain.

'Perhaps you'd like to go yourself?'

'I wish I could. But I'm committed to holing

180

up at Durham with my collaborator, we've run short of time for finishing the job,' I said and he consoled me with the thought:

'It's not quite the best time of year for South Africa of course.'

'I suppose not,' I agreed, thinking regretfully about *crux*—the Southern Cross, the smallest constellation in the sky, and Achernar, the brightest star in the long constellation of Eridanus, about beautiful constellar Carina, bright Canopus, Antares in Scorpius, Chamaleon, Circinus, Pavo and Grus—the names were like poetry in my mind. If Mr Paxton had tried to persuade me to go out there myself, deadline or not I'd have agreed. Instead, he told me he'd had previous dealings with a reputable firm of private investigators in Cape Town and if I agreed would commission them to make inquiries.

CHAPTER TWENTY

He is away again. I don't even know the address where he's staying, it is such a top-secret establishment. He left a contact number but said it was only for use in emergencies. I am not happy here without him but have never said so again, since the time he told me I was being silly in a tone of such disdainful surprise that I realise SHE would never have complained.

She's never mentioned. He does not say her name, there is no personal trace of her in the house, only the museum cases show she ever existed. But I feel her, all the time and more and more. When his long, smooth fingers touch my skin, I remember they touched hers first. When I fold his strong, lean body into my softness, was it in this way and thus? Did he stroke here and caress there? Is that where he learnt what to do? For he knows, oh so exactly. I've been subjugated. By day he's distant, speaks little, takes no part in my affairs or I in his, but later, ready, yearning for him in our bed, when I hear his study door close and his footsteps on the stair and he comes at last, then he's my love, my lover, my master. And I must be his alone. I have to know it's me he touches and kisses and—ah, even in this language nobody in my house and few people in my new country could read, I can't write the words for what he does. But she—did she utter them? Does he sense her, is it her body he enters, not mine?

How strange to remember when I didn't love him. He was the answer to my prayer, but it wasn't a prayer for love, only for a home and life and a future. I am a realist. We each needed what the other could give and I set myself to learn to please him, running his house as he liked, looking after him as a housekeeper would, in exchange for the roof over my head and his name. I remember, I remember. But now I cannot imagine what I remember. I cannot feel myself at a time when he was not all in all to me. And I dread that I am less than that, to him.

He must have loved her. Was he desolate when she died?

They met in China. He rescued her just before the war broke out, brought her home to 'safety' they thought. She could still be alive if she'd stayed in Shanghai. And he—no. He might have found another woman. And if he had, then I might never have met him that night in Cavendish Square. I went back there the other day, took the back door out of John Lewis's, my arms full of new material for my boudoir, and went to the very place, stood under the very lilac tree where I'd stood crying that evening and wishing, yes actually wishing that I was back in Budapest, when he came. Old, he seemed to me that day, a tall, thin, messily dressed elderly man.

How did he meet her? Was she a damsel in distress? No, she can't have been that, not with a child. I don't know anything at all about her, except that she was expert in oriental antiquities, for she collected all the chinoiserie in this house, it was shipped across the world for her. I hate it, all those cases full of treasures I have to dust and clean like a museum curator, with nervous care because everything is worth so much money. Perhaps one day he'll agree to sell it.

I wonder if she stole them? In the chaos of China during the 1930s there must have been ample opportunity for picking up treasures. What couldn't I have picked up at home [translator's

note: *home* crossed out, *Hungary* inserted]
myself, the buhl furniture, the Herendt porcelain,
if it had been possible to get it out? She was not
Chinese, she was Jewish. What made him turn to
such a woman?

I don't even know what she looked like. Her
son is large, dark, implacable. He doesn't speak
of her either, though perhaps he would if I knew
him better. He hardly comes here and when he
does, it's not as a son. B isn't interested in him,
as he is in Katarina and Christina. Those two, he
watches tumble about in a kind of scientific
wonderment. And that's also a kind of love.

CHAPTER TWENTY-ONE

Having met her party at Heathrow, a group of
'senior citizens' who had taken up a special
holiday offer (cheap, because it was not the
best season for Cape Town) in the *Argus*, Hilly
left them to sleep on the overnight flight.
Wakeful herself, she looked down on the
fabled coast of Africa and clocked the
numinous moment of crossing the equator. A
dark-suited, dark-skinned man from the local
agency met the party at the airport, conducted
the two dozen elderly travellers solicitously to
a coach and pointed out the zebras on the
hillside.

A pink hotel, a chintzy suite, a sunny

184

balcony with a view of a sugar-loaf mountain, a sparkling swimming pool, an elaborate buffet on a shady terrace. What more, one of the pax inquired, could you ask? Duty bound to look after them, Hilly was pleased to discover that on this first day the majority of them voted to rest. There was swimming in the hotel's pool, long chairs in the dappled shade of a scarlet-flowered tree, a buffet lunch. And by the time it got dark, a solid, impenetrable cloud had draped itself all over the mountain. 'It's the tablecloth,' Hilly told one of her charges. 'On Table Mountain, you see. Don't worry, it will be fine tomorrow.'

It wasn't fine, but for the next week the weather was just about good enough to do everything on the full, exhausting programme promised in the brochure. As one of the travellers remarked, they were certainly getting their money's worth. It was the beginning of the second week before Hilly was able to escape.

She hadn't seen Ari when he left the package she was to take his mother at the agency. He'd done it up in gift wrap and Hilly had argued with herself for ages about peeking. It would be a low thing to do, nosy and interfering. Then she thought about checking in. 'Has anyone given you a package, have you been with your case since it was packed?' In a way it was her duty to make sure that the contents were innocent. But it was very small, not much bigger or heavier than a book, there was no way this was a bomb. But what if customs and immigration asked her about it, she'd have to admit not knowing what was inside. Should she, shouldn't she, shall I, shan't I? She didn't, in the end, because it felt like snooping would break the fragile growth of her relationship with Ari. So as she sat in the taxi on the way to Oranjesicht, she clutched the gaudy parcel, untampered-with.

The quiet suburb was off the beaten tourist-track and Hilly had never been in the district before. The wide road ran straight up a gentle hill towards the cliff-like green face of the mountain. Some houses had driveways or paved front areas but the one the driver pulled up beside could hardly be seen behind a jungle of brilliant shrubs. There was a gate, rickety but firmly closed, to which were screwed two signs, a little plaque saying 'Peakview' and a red and white sign reading 'Armed Response'. Then Hilly saw that all the properties within sight bore similar warnings. If she stood here too long uniformed men with guns might screech to a halt beside her. She pressed a bell on the gatepost, wiped her damp forehead and pulled at her shirt to let air circulate under it. Her feet felt swollen in unsuitably heavy loafers. She pulled a comb through her hair, wanting to look poised for Ari's mother. But even after several rings, nobody answered the door.

Hilly tried to see through the cracks in the gate, but it was solidly backed with a sheet of metal. Then, realising that the driver was watching curiously, she walked along the fence. It was just possible to see the house through glossy leaves, a pleasant, Dutch Colonial single-storey building with gracefully curved eaves, white with black borders. But even from this distance and at this angle she could see it was in bad condition, paint peeling, some of the greenish roof tiles missing. Not much money around, then.

'Alloo!'

Hilly heard it several times before realising the shouts were for her. She turned to see the woman standing beside her own armed response warning placard. French, she thought, recognising the woman's nationality from her narrow, seemingly lidless brown eyes, her full mouth and her obvious sexual self-confidence, in spite of a truly ghastly combination of pink shorts, a lurex halter-neck top, gilt mules and bouffant red hair. Walking across the quiet road towards her Hilly saw deep-wrinkled leathered skin.

'Good morning, I wonder, do you know the lady who lives here?'

'*Qui?*'

'Mrs Lang?'

They conversed in this monosyllabic and uninformative fashion for a few minutes. A black maid (wearing, Hilly was surprised to see, old-fashioned uniform complete with starched, frilly apron) was summoned to join in, though her English was very limited. Then a battered Honda drew up, driven by an old, grizzled man in empire-building shorts.

'You asking about Emmy and Lenny?' he said. 'Can't tell you much, we keep ourselves to ourselves round here, it's one of the good things about it. Nosy people in Godalming.'

'Is that where you're from?' Hilly asked.

'Thirty-one years. When the wife passed on I came out to be near my sister. Should have done it years ago—look.' His gesture indicated the blue sky, the brilliant view of the mountain, and the black maid. 'This is the life.'

'I can see it must be.'

'No mealy-mouthed crap about servants either—this lot are grateful for the work here. Actually grateful!'

Luckily the maid had gone in, though Hilly realised she must often have heard similar remarks.

'Did you say there were several people living in that house?' she asked.

'There was a pair of them, Emm and poor old Lenny, they moved in just after I did.'

'Nice place.'

'It belongs to Mrs Fourie, when her husband died she moved out of town.' The old man went on, 'There's students living there now, they'll be out at college I daresay, good riddance, the rumpus they kick up in that pool till all hours is nobody's business.'

'How lovely, a pool.'

'We've all got those. Come and have a look if you like. Ron Phillips's the name.' Hilly said her own name, called to her driver that she'd be a little while and followed Ron across the road to another gabled bungalow and another, different-coloured notice about high security. This one's logo was a picture of a machine gun.

He was probably lonely. Nice to live in a lovely climate and landscape, and to have a maid to wait on you, no doubt nice to be unobserved—though to do what? Hilly wondered—but he would have had more friends in Godalming. Inside the house was purest home-counties, muted chintz which looked sadly wan in the strong light, as did a few wishy-washy water-colours and a beige close-carpet. The only thing in the large room bright enough for this new world was a school photo of grinning teenagers. 'Your grandchildren?' she murmured.

'Young tearaways the both of them. Tea?'

'Thanks, can I help make it?'

'No need. Sal, tea!' he suddenly bawled, adding, 'It's not her real name but that's unpronounceable.' His maid was not in pastiche uniform, instead she wore a T-shirt and jeans with trainers, but her attitude was deferential and nervous, and when he told her to put the tray outside Hilly could hear the cups rattling on their saucers. 'You have to keep them up to the mark.' Hilly thanked her with excessive politeness, aware it was pointless. What would civility do to alleviate the plight of a girl from one of the terrifying townships she'd herself, repeatedly, warned her charges to keep away from?

Most of the garden was taken up by a kidney-shaped pool full of greenish, slightly murky water. 'I don't use it much. Want a go?'

'No, thanks very much. I swam at the hotel this morning.'

'Where you staying?'

'The Mount Nelson.'

'Oh, very nice.' His attitude changed at that, as though that evidence of riches made Hilly more important than she'd seemed so far. 'You'll be looking round all the good spots then. Been up the mountain yet?'

'Yes, we went up in the cable car, wonderful view. And down the Cape.'

'Right, mustn't miss the Cape of Good Hope while you're here, and the Botanical Gardens, that's unique. And then there's the wine lodges—I've become quite knowledgeable about them so if you could do with a guide . . .'

'Oh, that is kind,' Hilly said insincerely. 'But we've got a full programme planned out already, you see.'

'You were asking about your friend.'

'My friend's mother, she's called Mrs

190

Marguerite Lang.'

'Not much I can tell you, we said good morning through the hedge and that was about it, people don't walk round here much and what with poor old Lenny . . .'

'Her companion? Was something wrong with her?'

'Had Alzheimer's, didn't she?'

'So Mrs Lang—Emmy—looked after her?' Hilly hadn't realised that Ari's mother was a carer, he hadn't mentioned it. Or anything else, really.

'Not a nice life, that, I know, I've seen it back home—well, you can't keep it up indefinitely, can you, what with the shouting and aggression, and then there's slops and mess—nappies—it would get a saint down.'

'It got so bad?'

'Like I said, I can't tell you exactly, you don't get to see your neighbours round here except waving from the car sometimes, and then I'd see Emm by the pool sometimes. She tried to keep Lenny away from it of course. Tried.' Hilly went over to his fence, a chain link affair thickly woven with brilliantly green and orange shrubs. Bougainvillaea, she thought, or hibiscus or frangipani or flame trees; all she knew about tropical plants was a list of evocative names. Between the leaves she could get a better view of Peakview. It looked more run-down than a few months' occupation by students could explain, with cracks on the walls and gaps, visible even from this distance, between windows and their frames, and paint peeling off the louvred shutters.

'Nice house,' she said.

'Mrs Fourie lived here, I've heard, all her married life. 'Course it was quite a posh district when she was young.'

'It looks quite posh now.'

'Not like some. You should see Kirstenbosch.'

'Yes, we went there.'

'So you know this isn't a patch on it. But there's a lot of us incomers in the district now, which suits me all right, and people like the Falaises over there who're just here for a few months, but the old Cape Towners, they've moved up the mountain or out to the sea.'

'I think it's lovely here,' Hilly said sincerely. 'This climate. . .'

'That what brought you out then?'

'No, I'm here on business, but I promised a friend I'd bring this to his mother. Mrs Lang.'

'But she's gone, didn't your friend know?'

'Gone?'

'No, not dead, I didn't mean that, but she left after poor old Lenny passed on. Sit down and I'll tell you about it.'

He's bored out of his mind, poor old chap, Hilly thought. He ushered her back to the white plastic chairs under his straw sun roof and began to talk.

They'd come down from Jo'burg together,

not all that long ago. Two years? Eighteen months? Made friends in some clinic, the Mary Rose Clinic? Margaret Rose, after the Little Princess? Something like that. Anyway, they'd met and chummed up and decided to move down to the Cape together, two lonely women. Emmy's partner had died, he'd been Spanish or Cuban, and Lenny was on her own too. She was failing already when they got here, but you couldn't have known how quickly it would go.

Lenny died in August. A merciful release, Ron said. She'd have had to go into a home else, what she needed was too much for one woman to supply, round the clock care—she'd escaped into the road once, wandering along half naked, couldn't even remember her own name—and heavy! You couldn't expect poor old Emm to go on heaving her in and out of bed, on and off the toilet—he'd seen it before. There came a point that you had to give in. Better dead, he said coldly. And added, 'Even like that.'

'Like what?

'Drowned, didn't she? Wandered out, well, she'd done it before, half-way down the road in her knickers before Emm could catch her, and this time into the pool she went. Floating face down like a sack stuffed with feathers.'

'Was it you that found her then?' Hilly asked.

'Saw her through the hedge, middle of the

morning. I won't lie to you, I didn't try to revive her.'

'How awful, it must have been absolutely traumatic for Mrs Lang, poor woman.'

'She was asleep. Exhausted, you can see why. She'd taken tablets, sleeping like the dead herself.'

Lenny O'Riordan was cremated at a private funeral and a few weeks later her companion had moved out. No, he didn't know where she'd gone and Hilly wasn't the first person to be asking, either, 'cos there'd been an inquiry agent from a firm in Cape Town only last week. He left his card, here it was, and he'd scribbled the name of the client on it in case Ron Phillips thought of anything that might help. The client lived in London. Hampstead, very nice part of the world. It was something to do with a legacy.

In the car on the way back to the hotel Hilly unwrapped Ari's package. It contained a box of inexpensive peppermint creams.

CHAPTER TWENTY-TWO

B is back from America. He has not brought presents for me or the girls, he's distracted and hardly greets or speaks to me. He sleeps in his dressing room! These Englishmen's dressing rooms, a bleak little box in which he can escape

194

from me. I put on the lace gown he brought from Geneva last year and walked through a cloud of the scent he bought in Paris when he was there after Christmas, and then I went in to him. I know I was soft and rosy and fragrant, how could he resist me unless there is someone else? Has he met another woman?

He is to see someone here in private. He will not tell me who it is. I am to take the girls to Portheglos three days early, he doesn't want me here. What's happening? Don't I have the right to know, who will be in my own home? He couldn't bring a woman here. Surely he could not do such a thing.

I ask if I should leave him food, refreshments for his visitor. No, he says, just go.

CHAPTER TWENTY-THREE

I arrived back from monastic seclusion in Durham. My colleague had left his wife to paint their new home while we indulged in the arcane pleasure of linguistic precision until, with one last heave, we finished the job. At home there was chaos, or crisis. Katie had used up the recording tape on my answering machine, though in the intervals between her calls there are some others, one from Mr Paxton's secretary asking me to ring back and one from Luke—*from Luke*! All he said was

'Hi' but that one syllable sounded in my head like the first crack of an avalanche before the icy walls come crashing down. I danced and pranced around, thrusting my clenched fists into the air, until remembering that Fidelis, on the floor below, would think I'd gone mad or got burglars.

He didn't leave his number, but the euphoria of hearing his friendly word got me through Katie's gulping hysteria. You wouldn't think she was a middle-aged woman. Not for the first time, I asked myself why I seemed to have taken responsibility for my cousin. What was it about her dependency and my practicality that had turned me into this exasperating woman's prop and stay? I must talk to Fidelis about it. Perhaps, her speciality being early maternal relationships, she would say it was all down to some failing on Elena's part; or on my mother Sheila's. But I would feel better able to follow such thoughts now that my own child had called. It certainly made me better able to take Bill calmly.

'The old lady says you know astronomy.'

For an instant I thought the boy's light, hoarse voice actually was Luke's. The disappointment was momentary. His having been in touch was enough.

I'd come towards my home from picking up some perishables in Hampstead High Street. I'd freewheeled down the hill and I slid off the saddle at my gate to find the boy called Bill

196

athwart the front door, his leg in plaster and an ugly slash (stitched, disinfected and exposed to the air) on his face.

'She says you know all about it.' He swung the bad leg aside as I hauled the bike up the steps. I leant it in the common lobby and turned back to say:

'Are you OK now?'

'Yeah yeah, it's cool, but what about—'

'Astronomy?'

'She said I should talk to you, it's for the general essay.'

'Yes, I know about general essays,' I said with feeling. 'My own son went through it all.' But Bill wasn't interested in that.

'The Net's full of stuff and I can do the maths, that's no prob, but I still don't get it about the eclipse. Have you ever seen one?'

'No, Bill, this is the first since 1927.'

'Can't be.'

'Visible in the UK, I mean. The last one was long before I was born, and the next won't be for more than seventy years, you might live to see it but I won't.'

'What about seeing them in other places?'

I pulled my rucksack off my back. 'Yes, there's been lots of them abroad, I can't remember where, d'you want to come up? I've got books about it.'

'No, I only want—just why it grabs you, know what I mean?'

I sat down on the doorstep beside him. It

was a sunny, sultry July morning, with blurred, motionless shadows. 'Imagine,' I said, gesturing towards the metallic glint of the sky, 'imagine the sun just going out.'

'Yeah, well, it does that every night.'

'Listen, this is what'll happen, at the eleventh minute of the eleventh hour of the eleventh day of August.' I couldn't stop my voice sounding portentous. 'The first thing will be when the moon cuts a notch in the disc of the sun. The light will lessen. The atmosphere will get dull and grey. They say the birds go to roost and flowers fold their petals and dogs howl, and people howl too, if they're superstitious, it's so scary. Then if you're high enough up to see it the moon's shadow will zoom across at supersonic speed, it'll be wonderful over the sea, and then you see the stars, right in the middle of the morning. And there'll be beads of light all twinkling round the sun, like a diamond ring in the dark sky. You are standing in the shadow of the moon, like you're in my shadow now. And all round the horizon there's an eerie yellow twilight, and you can see gas clouds in the sun's edges, everyone that's ever seen a total eclipse says it's terrifying and wonderful. I can't wait.'

'It won't be like that in London.'

'It won't get completely dark but even here you'll have the shadow across the sun.'

He said, 'Big deal' but not aggressively. I promised to find him some stuff he could use

198

in his essay, but I realised the first thing to do was get down to Addison Road. It was a beautiful day. I sailed down from Hampstead in the soft sunshine, great wafts of delicious scent from beds of roses assailed my sense of smell as I passed through the cherished gardens of St John's Wood, Little Venice and Notting Hill. The long established trees of Addison Road glistened in the morning sun.

Katie, soft, seeming, inexplicably, a little damp, and panting, fell on my neck (why isn't it round my neck? Or on my bosom?).

The police had been. 'An inspector called,' I murmured flippantly.

'Yes, Detective Inspector somebody or other, his card's in the fruit dish for you to ring him, and that Constable Hicks. They wanted—' Her words came out in a kind of gasp. 'Victoria, they wanted to search the house!'

'Whatever for?'

'It was something to do with that skeleton, the man they found up the road under a patio.'

'They wanted to search this house because of that body? For heavens' sake, why?'

'They didn't say, but I wouldn't let them in.'

'How could you stop them?' I asked, impressed.

'I rang Mr Paxton and he said they'd need a search warrant, or they'd have to get your permission, and they said surely I wouldn't mind, the place was half empty as it is, and I said it was an impertinence and it felt all wrong and it was out of the question and please would they go away, and so they did.'

'Well done, Katie, I am impressed.'

'It was rather, wasn't it, I was quite proud of myself.'

'But Katie, why did you mind so much? What harm would it have done?'

'There's something very heavy, very portentous, about it all, the very thought is full of horror and misery and I couldn't let that contamination infect my home. Something was telling me not to, I felt it very strongly. And then Gayle came—'

'What was she doing here?

'Well, I'd spoken to Christina at Portheglos and she spoke to Gayle. She came round to make sure I wasn't getting the family involved with anything messy. She's doing something with her business—opening it to the public, could that be what she said?'

'Taking it public. Floating it on the Stock Exchange.'

'Yes, something that means its reputation's all important so she doesn't want the name Kittermaster mixed up with anything at all dubious. Well, none of us do, for that matter.'

'Making the police get a search warrant might not be the most sensible course, in that case.' I went downstairs, fished the inspector's card out of a bowl of apricots, rang him up and made an appointment for him to come round. He wouldn't tell me why he wanted to so I said, 'Are you looking everywhere round here?' and when he didn't reply I went and called at a few of the neighbouring houses. During the middle hours of the day not all had anyone at home. Next door was the property of a South American embassy and it didn't seem worth asking them, and on the other side a Slavic au pair only understood enough of the question to go pale at the word 'police'. I did eventually speak to the owners of two other houses in the street, neither of which had aroused official interest—though you could see that every inch had been modernised and poshed up, so there couldn't be any evidence left from forty years back.

I'd told Katie that ours was the only house within miles where there might still be anything from those days and that must be why they were interested in it, but it wasn't that. Detective Constable Hicks let it out. They were 'acting on information received.' What information, received from whom? They wouldn't say. Nor would they say what they were looking for. Three unmarked cars and a squad car had parked outside number 447. A whole team had come to search the house, women with clipboards, men in disposable overalls (coveralls?), assistants carrying wads of clear plastic containers. All this for a decades-old death? My optimistic mood rapidly evaporated. Something serious (Luke would say 'heavy') was going on here.

Katie had gone out for the afternoon, heeding my slightly self-interested warning; whatever was about to happen would seem much worse with her firing off a chorus of omens throughout. And in fact, even for me, practical and unimaginative as I am, it was not pleasant to see these strangers taking over. I'd been prickled once or twice before, when showing prospective purchasers round, on seeing them fling open doors and drawers as though they had a right to; but that was as nothing to standing by while floorboards were prised up (and, to do the police justice, put back into place again), panels tapped, veneers unscrewed and plumbing probed. And it wasn't even my own old home.

It would have been easier if I'd had the faintest idea what they were searching for. A weapon? What weapon could possibly be identified after forty years? A further identification? Was that why one woman officer was making such a careful examination of the photographs in Elena's boudoir?

They didn't even want coffee. Too restless to sit down, I went out to the paved terrace to drink mine on the roof, remembering sitting here with Elena at her properly laid tea table. Paxton had faxed on to me his inquiry agent's report. The preamble was in formal, pompous language, the kind of prose it offends me to read. I forced my eyes down the flimsy page.

The detective had written his conversations

down verbatim, beginning with a nursing home in Johannesburg, the Rosemary Clinic, where Marguerite Lang had made friends with Lenny O'Riordan. An administrator remembered the two women well. 'Emm' Lang (Emm? I noticed incredulously) was recovering from a hip replacement operation. She'd met Lenny while she was there as an in-patient. Lenny would come round to this and other such establishments, to do the patients' hair. A smart-looking woman, sharp as a pin, the administrator thought, mid-fifties maybe? She and Emm had quite a bit in common, Brits by birth, well-travelled, they'd lived in half a dozen countries between them in their time but lonely now, the both of them. The administrator had been pleased for them when the two chummed up. You'd hear them in Emm's room, telling each other their life stories, laughing and joking around. Then Emm got better and Lenny gave in her notice, they'd decided to move down to Cape Town together. No, she hadn't kept in touch after that, well, you couldn't, could you, not with the number of old dears that came through these doors in a year.

The inquiry agent went to the address he'd been given in Cape Town but found that Lenny O'Riordan had died and Emm Lang had moved away without leaving a forwarding address.

Constable Hicks came out to ask if I had a

key to the wine cellar.

'It's not locked, you just have to turn the handle in a special way. I'll come.'

'No hurry, madam, finish your drink.'

'Mr Hicks, I wish you'd explain what this is all about. What's going on here is far beyond any routine check, there must be some reason to be pulling the place to pieces.'

And that was when he told me they were acting on information received.

'Can't you tell me more than that? Oh, come on, Mr Hicks, you know anything that happened so long ago can't possibly be anything to do with me, still less with my cousins.'

He looked fatherly. 'I can see it's uncomfortable for you, madam.'

'No, but it's peculiar. I'd really like to have some idea—what information? Received from whom?'

'I really can't say.'

Another woman might have got more out of him by fluttering and flirting. I didn't even know how to try, so got up to go in the house and show them how to open the cellar door. I watched from the top of the stairs as every wine rack was moved aside. 'Pity the booze has gone,' I heard one man say, from the chilly depth. The wine was the first thing to go after my uncle died.

Elena had sent all Bertram's specials to be auctioned at Christie's. Rum was her own preferred tipple.

'There's cracks across this floor.'

'Subsidence,' I shouted down. 'That's what the surveyor said, anyway.' It didn't stop them levering a couple of flagstones up, to find, as I could have told them, undisturbed London clay.

Later, much later, I was making up my mind to leave them to it. Surely, I thought, this is beyond the call of an executor's duty? The searchers, working their way upwards, had reached the attics and I followed them to make a final check. It was warm under the roof, on a day like this, the air still but full of dust mites, and with shapes of dirt on the floorboards where the garbage sacks had rested; I noticed something I'd missed, a tiny teddy bear wearing hand-knitted clothes, wedged into the corner of a roof beam. A man in latex gloves riffled neatly through a box of old lace and linen, opened and closed the dolls' house doors, tapped the copper water cylinder. Then he came to the old suitcases, still waiting for me to order a skip. The empty ones and the case of gloves, the canvas case of men's clothes I'd found all those weeks ago.

'Sir.'

'Those must have been my uncle's things,' I said. 'It's all waiting for a skip.'

'Look, sir.' He held up a pair of trousers. They were small, narrow and very short.

'I saw Sir Bertram Kittermaster once,' the

Inspector said from behind me. 'He was a local celebrity. Wasn't he very tall?'

'Yes, he was,' I agreed. 'Those clothes weren't his after all. They couldn't ever have belonged to him.'

CHAPTER TWENTY-FOUR

I have done it. I can hardly believe it of myself. How could I act in a manner that my husband and all his family would so little understand, far less forgive? Brought up in their courteous, honourable England to be gentlemen and ladies, kind to the weak, courageous against aggressors, their words their bonds—well, that is not what the life I learnt was like. How disdainfully I have heard them speak of those who don't come up to their standards of behaviour, excepting only Sheila, she is humbled by life. But not so Betty, with her bouncing, pony-mad extrovert daughter the domineering Gayle, a Kittermaster woman par excellence in the making. Susan, finicky and precise. Olive, so bound up in her 'good works' that she's blind to daily life. These Kittermaster women, cold and calm as ice, I can never be like them. They treat me politely. We are invited to dine, for Bertram, however uncommunicative, is a famous catch for any dinner table; I'm just the wife. Betty gave a ladies' luncheon for me when Christina was a baby. Half a dozen blonde or mousy beanpoles and me, small, round, foreign. I shall always be an outsider in their company.

And the men, all so clever and sure of themselves. I once read a long poem by an American called Alice Duer Miller who wrote about her love for this country and the husband who represented it for her. Bertram said it was pap. But like her I feel that 'I have married England.' English, however, I shall never be. I have my precious passport, my nationality is safe, but my true self, my inner person, the essence of me can never match the outward show. The marks of my own formative experiences are too strong. I am untrustful.

Why do I bother to record this excuse in a language nobody here can read for no other eyes than mine to see?

Because I'm ashamed of sneaking and snooping. I have been infected by Englishness at least thus far. No, I'm proud too. I am right to protect my interests. And what real woman made of flesh and hot blood could go incuriously off to Portheglos leaving him to—to do what? The thought of a woman in my bed is such anguish that I feel it in my stomach, the pain is like a knife piercing me. I can't let it happen. This I cannot do. He tells me to leave him in the house alone and I must know why. That is, for whom.

He is mine.

I will not let another woman have him, not for a single moment. Too much has been taken from me already.

So I took the children to Portheglos. The train, the taxi. And I told the taxi to return for me. It is the Easter school holidays, cold, windy English weather, but all the other wives are there too, and Sheila's child Victoria is staying in our cottage, inward, quiet, always, I think, a little frightened. Olive's benevolence stretches to me. I lied, fluent, persuasive. Lying is natural to one who grew up where I did, when I did.

An appointment in Harley Street; a feminine ailment, the suggestion of something doom-laden, of which my husband will have to learn if it's true, but which I'm protecting him from meanwhile. 'No need to worry him if it's all a false alarm,' Olive agrees. 'A stiff upper lip, that's the ticket, well done, Elena.' She sounds a little surprised that I have shown such restraint, and is right to be so, for if I really had a serious illness or even a less serious one, naturally I would discuss it with my husband immediately. That's what marriage means. But I didn't say so to Olive. She will look after the girls while I go back to London. 'They'll be all right, don't worry about them. Good luck.' Correct, kind, oh so English. My own aunts and cousins would have wept and embraced me, warm and emotional, sharing my pain.

I took the milk train and was back at Paddington by mid-morning.

Ridiculous to approach my own house in secrecy. I don't know how to set about it. I should have planned it better. I can't just walk up the road. Too many people know me. He might see me.

I go to a telephone box. Our number rings nine times, and then it is not he but Mrs Beck who answers. He must be out. I put the receiver down without speaking and press Button B to retrieve my coins. What shall I do? I feel displaced in London, lost, almost hunted. It is four and a half years since I felt the sensation but the fear of discovery floods back. Ridiculous, I tell myself, this isn't Buda in 1956, I'm in London, it's a free country and I belong here. I shall go home. To my house.

But I feel as furtive as I did that October, leaving home with so very little, tiny necessities tied in a cloth and fastened under my jacket so as to make sure Papi wouldn't suspect anything. And there was Mammi, almost pushing me away. 'Go, Elena, go, there may never be another chance, take it now while you can.' She was forcing herself not to cry, but moisture lay like dew in the deep wrinkles under her eyes.

I went to Addison Road but found myself closing the gate softly and tiptoeing up the path. I could see below, Mrs Beck ironing at the kitchen table with her back to me. She's getting deaf. I let myself gently into the house. Odd, not to call immediately for my babies, 'Katie, Christina, Mummy's home.' There was no sound.

What should I do? Say 'Mrs Beck, it's me, I'm back'?

Oh, she'd say. Oh madam, what a surprise,

209

you gave me quite a turn.

I walked upstairs, silent on the thick red carpet we laid last year, my hands sliding on the smooth handrail, breathing in the familiar smells. Furniture polish, Brasso, woodsmoke from the drawing-room and acrid coal in the kitchen range. Was I sweating? I'd smelt my own fear during those days of escape.

But this was not my own body odour. Marlene was in my bedroom, preening herself in front of my own pierglass in my own fur coat. Two of my own dresses lay on the bed. Her feet were in my own crocodile shoes, my own pearls hung round her filthy neck.

She looked surprised to see my reflection behind hers but not dismayed. It came to me that she'd done this many times before, as familiar with my belongings as I was, making free, prowling round my house, snooping, watching.

She held my gaze as she calmly removed my things, flinging, them in a heap on the floor. She put on her own clothes, that hideous school uniform into which the English cram their adolescent girls. I hadn't said anything and she knew I wouldn't if I wanted to retain her grandmother's services. Her expression I recognised. Just so had the young soldiers looked, when they grabbed the titbits they wanted from our home and flung the others to the floor. So too, the policemen who helped themselves to the meat in the butcher's stall or the eggs for which we had queued for so many hours. It was the gaze of indifferent power. Might is right, is the English phrase.

So now I am sitting in my boudoir, alone and wafting and silent. Waiting for him. And for whom?

CHAPTER TWENTY-FIVE

The police gave me receipts for everything they took away. I was standing in the hall, leaning against the faded green wallpaper while awkwardly signing the carbon copies on a hand held clipboard, when the bell rang and a pocket-Venus of a woman police constable opened the door. Gayle looked her most formidable, the image of the high-flying professional woman in her perfectly tailored black suit, with high heels, vibrant hair and an expression of hauteur.

'Just what is going on here?' she demanded.

'Oh Gayle. Inspector, this is my cousin—'

'Gayle Kittermaster,' she said briskly. 'And you are?

'Gayle, this gentleman's from the Notting Hill police—'

She interrupted again. 'Have you got a search warrant?'

'Gayle, they didn't need one, I said they could—'

'You let them in, Victoria? Without your

lawyer present? Inspector, what's the name of your superior? A formal complaint should be made. This is unacceptable behaviour.'

'I was under the impression that Mrs Merton has the authority to grant us entry, madam. If that isn't the case, of course—'

Moving politely past us the occupying army took their booty out of the house. They had aroused local interest. An au pair with a buggy and a uniformed nanny with a pram were watching from the pavement. And a car with a sticker advertising the *Kensington and Chelsea Chronicle* was parked in front of the saloon car towards which the Detective Inspector was walking.

Gayle began, 'If one single word appears in the media—'

I spoke simultaneously and, for the first time in my life, more forcefully than Gayle. 'What happens here is up to me until the estate's wound up, and I gave permission.'

'Well, why, what's this all about, what brought you here in the first place?' she demanded.

'They say they're acting on information received,' I told her.

'What about, for God's sake? What kind of investigation is this?'

'I'm investigating a murder, madam.'

'That long-lost skeleton?'

'The murder of Dr Tomo Matsuzakara, madam, who died on or before a date in 1961.'

'Who was he?'

'He was an American of Japanese descent, madam, who was reported as a missing person from his hotel in London in April 1961.'

'But why here, why this house?'

He repeated the mantra about information received, and I watched as Gayle did a transformation trick. How did she make her whole outline soften and her eyes become so appealing? What trick turned her into something I could never be, a woman men fall for? It wasn't just her words, which echoed my own earlier plea.

'But did someone ring, an anonymous call? Or letter? Someone who'd got an old grudge against the family? Oh, do give me a clue, Mr Hicks.' Needless to say Gayle's wiles worked; they always do.

'There was a letter.'

'A letter!'

'An informant saw something suspicious back then.'

'An informant? D'you know who?'

'The letter wasn't signed.'

'An anonymous letter, I might have guessed.' Suddenly she was contemptuous and unyielding. 'So on the strength of an anonymous letter, probably from some nutter, you've torn this place to pieces, wasted police time—and—' (anyone could tell that this was what really mattered to Gayle) 'you simply don't begin to realise what damage you've

213

done. If this gets into the nationals . . . !'

The car from the local paper had moved off. With any luck the story would go no further and Gayle, who lived in a different part of London, would never see it.

'What's this you're taking away, what's in these boxes? That suitcase.'

'Gayle, don't. Look, I've got receipts. Let it be.'

She stood seething beside me while the car-boots were loaded and until the police had driven away. Then, slamming the door, she turned on me. 'I can't believe you did this thing, Victoria, you must be completely bonkers. Didn't Katie tell you what I said?'

'Yes, she told me.'

'You realise this will revive that libel about Bertram being a traitor.'

'I don't see how a Japanese American skeleton could be connected with spying for the Russians.'

'You're so naïve, don't you understand anything about public relations at all? Think what this'll do to the name. It's all right for you, you never were a real Kittermaster, but my whole reputation depends on it.'

'Bad luck.'

Gayle held out the little stack of receipts. 'Look how much they've taken, cases, boxes, it's unbelievable. Can't you see what this is going to look like?'

'I don't know what this fuss is about, Gayle,

214

it's hardly going to affect your flotation, it's not connected at all.'

'A murder investigation? Are you kidding?'

'A murder that happened thirty-eight years ago, it's nothing to do with you, or me or any of us.'

Making another of her swift changes, she said in a gentler tone, 'What d'you think it's all about, Vicky? God, isn't it gloomy here?'

'The kitchen's about the only habitable room left.'

We went down together. Gayle wrinkled her nose. 'I smell damp. Or dry rot. Or worse.'

I began to fill the kettle. 'I know, I only wish we could get rid of the place and be done with it. God knows how long it'll take to sort things out with Marguerite Lang and meanwhile Katie seems set on staying here.'

'You'd have thought she could clean it up a bit then.' Katie had stuck what she called star charts to every vacant patch of wall and a multi-faceted witch ball hung from a ceiling hook. But there were cobwebs in the corners, and mouse droppings near the skirting boards. Gayle said, 'No tea, I want a drink, after that.'

'I suppose there might be something,' I said dubiously.

'Oh really, this place!' She began searching the cupboards, making little noises of disgust at the less savoury crannies, until eventually finding a bottle of red plonk at the back of the dresser. I recognised it as one I'd once brought

Elena. It may have been beneath Gayle's usual quality standards but was quite up to mine, and after she had washed and polished two glasses, we sat peaceably sipping. 'Remember drinking gin out of tooth glasses in the old boathouse?' she said.

Yes, I remembered, both the taste and the terror that made me swallow the fiery liquid (I've hated gin ever since) and the recognition of that same fear in my son's eyes when, too late, I discovered what he'd been doing in the summer holidays.

It was my first summer at Portheglos for many years. Luke was ten, and we were invited to stay by Gayle because she said my son mustn't miss out on the defining Kittermaster experience. For some conventional or insincere reason, I thought he'd love it, a town kid transported to the dream country. Stuart wouldn't come ('You don't expect me to waste my vacation on your snobby cousins?'), so Luke and I went down by train and bus and taxi. By the late 1980s, long after the Beeching axe had felled branch lines and the Thatcher squeeze decimated bus routes, Portheglos had become almost inaccessible by public transport and my memory, possibly inaccurate, is of a ten-or eleven-hour journey.

Gayle's share at Portheglos consisted of the house she'd inherited (being an only child) from her father. He, the son of an eldest son, had been allotted one of the better properties there, a square stone cottage in a shallow, slightly sheltered hollow. It had originally been built for a gamekeeper. Gayle's friend Lucinda, the wife of a junior minister, was there with her four children and so was Bo Kittermaster with her two Etonian sons. I shared an attic bedroom with a German au pair girl, and Luke was put in a downstairs room, once a game larder and later lined with triple stacks of wooden bunks. Children at Portheglos lived in a private world of gangs, teams, secrets and adventures. The mothers conformed to an equally traditional pattern.

The others, like Gayle, had progressed gradually through the milestones of kids' bucket and spade holidays, Famous Five style adventures, surfing at the local resort, flirting in the neighbouring pubs, baby-sitting for older cousins, romantic cliff walks, and on to bringing their own babies. I'd missed out on the annual Portheglos experience. It was at once reassuring and frightening to find myself whisked into the next generation, suddenly exchanging one kind of boredom alternated with social unease for another.

By the 1980s, in Gayle's house, everything was high-tech. No more hand-pumped water or candle-lit evenings, no more juggling of bottled gas cylinders or refitting paraffin wicks. The whole estate was connected to mains services by that time and Gayle had installed banks of expensive equipment. But the rocky beach looked exactly as it had in the amateurish water-colours my great-great grandmother produced at the turn of the century, with clumps of mothers encamped on a flat rock with rugs and picnic baskets and skinny children in swimsuits cowering in the sea. A painting done by Edna Kittermaster in 1940 shows an identical scene. She'd been evacuated to Portheglos but (as her biography says) couldn't stand the undiluted company of women and children, went off to join the Special Operations Executive, having learnt perfect French when living in Paris before the war, was dropped into France and was captured and killed there. There's no premonition of her bitter fate in the sunny painting that now hangs in the Tate.

It was sunny the summer I took Luke there too. I remember beach picnics and starlit barbecues. I must have been mad, or bad, not to remember that the children would be in a different world. I didn't know anything about the bullying, teasing and initiation rituals Luke was put through until years later. He didn't seem much quieter than usual, always quite a subdued child, being our only one and with slightly impaired hearing. I just noticed that his thin body looked brown and well and attributed the shadows under his eyes to midnight feasts.

I couldn't have provided any protection even if I'd had the sense or sensitivity to realise Luke needed it. But now I wonder whether that was the moment when he began to lose faith in me.

I told Gayle, 'I'll be at Portheglos this year.'

'When?'

'For the eclipse.'

'Oh God, we've all got to have a family pow-wow about that, there's going to be hundreds of people as it is, all the kids' friends in tents and every bed on the estate spoken for. Couldn't you make it a different week, it's not as though you've got to come during school holidays.'

'Gayle!'

'What?'

'You're not suggesting I miss the total eclipse?'

'Well, it's not such a—'

'Yes it is,' I interrupted assertively. 'I've been looking forward to it for years.'

'Well, if you're sure.' She filled our glasses. 'This stuff is pretty disgusting but it's growing on me. Is there anything to eat?'

I found a tin full of Katie's home-made biscuits, spicy, star-shaped and stodgy. Gayle took one bite, ran her palm over her flat stomach and put the biscuit down. 'Now then,' she said, 'what do we make of this information received then? 1961, that's thirty-eight years ago, at least they can hardly suspect any of us of anything.'

'Katie and Christina were toddlers, but

you'd have been thirteen and I was eleven, we were quite old enough to have seen something and remembered it. And written an anonymous letter.'

'What, when the body turned up and it turned into a murder investigation? You're probably right. Do you remember anything fishy going on?'

'What kind of thing? All I recall about coming here was being sent out in the garden and made to look after the little girls while my mum gossiped with Elena. We never saw Bertram, he didn't join in. As for anything suspicious—what would it have been, that didn't seem worth mentioning at the time?'

'No doubt you'd remember seeing someone digging a grave.'

I said, 'Wouldn't someone have noticed the victim himself? There can't have been many Japanese men round here in 1961, London wasn't multiracial and multicultural in those days.'

'I dunno, Vicky, didn't the Indian High Commissioner live round here? I have a feeling his daughters went to my school.'

I've always felt a twinge whenever Gayle mentioned her education at a fiercely academic London day school. When we were children it was pure inferiority, since the establishment where my mother and I lived and worked was simply not in the same league. After that it was jealousy. If I'd been sent to St

Paul's like Gayle, I might have taken science and maths and done astronomy at university.

I said, 'But surely not Japanese people, Gayle, they must still have been post-war pariahs at that time, surely.'

'So someone might remember seeing him come to this house? D'you suppose that's what the cops were told?'

'It's possible,' I said, visualising the exclusive, imperial calm of the district in my childhood. 'The fact is, leave aside who told them to search here but once they'd come, I think those policemen did find something here.'

'All that stuff they took away. What was it?'

'Junk, mostly, things I'd put out for burning. But there was one case of men's clothes that I'd found when I was sorting the attic. They can't have been Bertram's, too small, and they looked like the right period, it was fifties gear.'

'Why the hell didn't you get rid of it right away then?'

'For God's sake, Gayle.' I felt righteously indignant. 'Just what do you think could have made me guess they might have belonged to a man who was murdered and buried up the road? And even if I had guessed, why would I have wanted to hide them? We're not trying to cover up a crime here, are we? I mean, come on, you don't seriously suppose that Bertram killed him?'

'Don't be silly, of course not.'

221

'Well then?'

'The media will bring his name into it.'

'The *Kensington and Chelsea Chronicle*—that's not going to affect your share price, Gayle.'

'Get real, Vicky, the minute the Kittermaster name appears every single newspaper and television and radio news channel will be on to it like vultures. It's only a matter of time, I'm surprised the Notting Hill police haven't sold the story already. And that's what I'm worried about.'

'At this delicate juncture.'

'I don't know what gives you the right to be so superior, Vicky, if you'd staked as much on your own business as I've done on mine—'

'OK, sorry, I do understand.'

'So sharpen your wits, Vicky, you've spent months nosing into all this mess, surely it's occurred to you? It certainly will to anyone else who knows about him. It all coincides, don't you see? He dropped out just about then. He had access to this house. I've no idea what connection he had with a Japanese American, I know nothing else about the whole affair, but one thing's blindingly obvious. Justin Lang was the person to blame.'

222

CHAPTER TWENTY-SIX

He has come back to the house, JL is with him. I do not call out, they don't know I'm in my little boudoir, I am afraid to admit it. How angry he will be.

I hear steps running down to the kitchen, then smell the food. I bought all that food, I carried the bacon back from the high street grocer, my little girls took the eggs from the egg-woman at the kitchen door. My rye bread from the delicatessen, my tomatoes from the greengrocer in Earls Court Road. I could smell every ingredient of the 'fry-up' (as Mrs Beck would call it) being cooked in my kitchen by that boy.

'Bertram,' he has called. 'Grub's up.' Bertram goes down the stairs. He has never eaten at the table down there throughout my time in this house. I set out the lace mats and silver candlesticks on polished walnut. He prefers to keep standards up. They are due to him.

Did SHE give him meals down there, is this how he lived with HER?

*   *   *

Later, in the train.

I tiptoed down to the hall and into the dining-room. The brass handle turned silently as I closed myself into the room. It's heavily quiet in there, the carpets and upholstery swallow sounds. One day he'll let me redecorate. I'd like clean parquet floors and central heating, grey walls without these Chinese water-colours he says are so valuable. This room is still HERS.

I eased up the sliding door of the serving hatch.

In my upbringing I had to learn sneaky tricks, as B's cousins would call them, overgrown schoolgirls that they are, sometimes when we are together at Portheglos I wonder how they would have coped with the dangers I grew up with, they know nothing of fear or secrecy. They are indomitable, these English women, in many ways, but I do not imagine Sheila or any of the others bending into the shaft of the food lift up from the kitchen, to eavesdrop on anyone. I did. My mouth was watering at the food smell and my heart thudding with anxiety. If he should find me here . . .

They were talking about B's American trip. B said he had to tell J about it. For your mother's sake, he said. I clutched on to the food serving shelf and stopped myself from rushing down to hammer my fists on to his chest and cry out— what of HER? Is SHE still the one?

But he didn't talk any more about her, he was describing the American laboratory where he'd been on his last trip, a mutual exchange of interally expertise, he called it.

'Don't tell me, this is all classified,' J interrupted. 'I may have signed the Official

224

Secrets Act but this is too—'

'But I must tell you.' B sounded anguished and I realised something dreadful was wrong. It hurt me to hear his voice like that. 'All the time there and all the way back, I've agonised over it.'

'The work, you mean?'

How does he dare, that boy, to ask him about his work? I would never venture.

'You know what they are doing there—well, we are as much involved as the Yanks are, developing those weapons. The allies have to make them to break them.'

'I understand that much,' J said. 'You lot at Porton, if you can't manufacture the stuff you couldn't produce its antidote, that's clear enough. Of course the risk's real enough, not just accident but once the weapons are in our hands—well, it will take a strong government to resist using them. That's where people like you come in.'

Is that exactly what he said? I repeat the conversation over to myself. The compartment is full, four people on each side, and my neighbour leans over to whisper, 'Are you all right, dear?' My lips must have been moving as I write. I tilt my notebook away—suppose she could after all read Hungarian—and say I'm very well.

Bertram was speaking of something else, he was back to HER. When he met her. I've never known this. It didn't sound as though J had either. Bertram was describing a hospital laboratory in China. SHE was working there, an

225

assistant. He went to her apartment, met her eight-year-old son. J is 31 now so it was 1938.

J spoke very quietly, I could only just hear. 'Did she know about her husband already? About my father?'

Know what? I thought. What was to know?

'Yes,' Bertram said, 'by then she'd heard, we all had, we knew what was going on in Manchuria, that's why we were working so furiously to develop our own protection at the time. I brought her here, Justin, but you should know she came for your sake in the end, it was a hard decision, she felt she was abandoning him. Pearl was not one to run away, without you she might even have gone back and tried to save him.'

They stopped talking and I heard the cutlery and crocks clattering. It was very cold in the dining-room and I looked longingly at the coals, laid ready to light. Then came a strong smell of coffee and the sound of the bubbling percolator. It's not good for him, it makes his heart palpitate.

'You've read about Manchuria, Justin, you know about—'

'How my father must have died in Pingfan, no better than a log of wood. Yes, I know.'

'Shiro Ishii.'

'Yes, I know the name.'

'And Okuda. Saburo Okuda.'

'His assistant.'

'I met him,' B says. 'I met him once in Japan,

226

long before it all began we were working in the same field, when I was a research student in Tokyo and science hadn't been perverted into what men like him made it. Justin, I met him. He was clever and sharp but full of prejudice. He spoke of people in the same way as the Nazis were already doing in Germany. He believed some were sub-human. Jews. He'd worked in Munich in the early thirties himself and become as infected with anti-Semitic feeling as it was possible to be. Rotten with it. To think of those benighted souls in his power when he was promoted to work with Ishii, no, better not to think. But when his name came out after the war and they said he'd died, I remembered him and hoped he was rotting in hell, Justin, for Pearl's sake, and Jacob's, whom I never knew, and yours because you never knew him, and for your people's sake, and for science itself, perverted and misused. It was my personalised, personal prayer.'

I never knew that B prays. He doesn't go to church. So many things I haven't been allowed to know about him.

'I hope your prayer has been answered, Bertram,' J said. He sounded gentle. Intimate. They are fond, the one man of the other, I had not known it before.

'No.' B's voice sounded—what? As hard to tell misery from glee, as it would be to know, from outside a room, whether his grunt at climax is pleasure or pain. But this was anguish. He

227

needed me then to comfort him but I dared not go down. He said, 'It has not been answered. I saw him. He is alive. He is working in America. They have acquired his services.'

'Alive? How can he be? It's not possible, you've made a mistake.'

Now B spoke coldly, objectively, as I've heard him with his colleagues, exchanging chilly facts and inferences devoid of feeling. 'He was at the laboratories. He has been given a new identity. He is a respected scientist, working with colleagues. They value him highly. They are sending him to Porton next week.'

I heard them begin to come upstairs and I shrank back behind the door. I could just hear the rest of their conversation. Justin asked if this man had realised B knew who he was and B said he was sure he had not. Orientals were used to Europeans not being able to tell them apart, and B said he'd been careful himself not to give his own emotion away, I kept a poker face, he said.

There were the sounds of putting on coats. I heard no more as B left the house with J, slamming the front door behind them. I waited until they must have walked as far as the main road and left myself.

I still don't understand what they were talking about but at least now I know it was not for another woman he wanted me out of the way, not even for one who is long since dead. I ought, I think, to be glad. And I am on the way back to my children.

228

CHAPTER TWENTY-SEVEN

It was sultry as only big cities can be. My upper arms stuck to my sides, my thighs stuck together. And I'm not even fat. Biking was fine while one was moving, the air felt cooling, but then it seemed even hotter when one stopped. I was counting the days till I could leave for Portheglos. Christina hadn't been as welcoming as she might at the prospect of fitting me into the cottage she and Katie jointly owned. She mentioned all the difficulties—her children, their friends, her own friends, Katie and all her mystical gear. The whole place would be jammed, she'd warned. Roads impassable, queues everywhere, shortages in the supermarkets. 'Unless you've booked your seat you'll never get on a train,' she said optimistically and sounded a little dashed when I told her I'd booked it months before. She warned me about water shortages, power cuts, gangs of illicit ravers, the biggest movement of population in peacetime ever. Was I really sure I wanted to come?

I'm not usually pushy. In any other circumstances I'd do almost anything rather than force myself in where I wasn't wanted. I knew every spare bed at Portheglos would be occupied in the second week of August, as would every other available bed, camping pitch and area of floor space in the county. All the media had been full of dire prophecies for weeks now; the far south-west was being prepared for siege conditions. And now the government's Chief Medical Officer of Health had issued a warning to everyone to stay at home and watch the eclipse on television, for fear of looking at the sun and being blinded for life.

Nonetheless, just this once I wasn't going to back off. Katie and Christina owed me, I implied without putting it into words. The least they could do was have me to stay this August. 'Oh well, if you insist,' Christina conceded. I had a train seat booked for Monday and with London so hot was counting the days.

Fidelis was in our shared front garden when I got home. She was wearing yellow sandals and a rust-coloured dress made of some multi-pleated, opaque material which made me realise my T-shirt and denim skirt wouldn't do; but then, Fidelis's clothes always had that effect on me and I never did anything about it. She'd been talking to Bill, out of plaster now. He said:

'Hi, Mrs M, I got the info about eclipses.'

'Oh, did you, Bill? That's good.'

'There's this geezer goes all over the world to catch them, the Caribbean last year and Hawaii before that, and India and China and the Philippines and New Guinea and lots of places.'

I'd known all that, having perused the lists of places where total eclipses had ever been and would be visible. That must be why Bill's recitation rang a muffled bell in my mind. But there was something else, surely? No, I couldn't catch on to the memory. I asked Bill, 'Has it made you want to see it?'

'It'll be on TV.'

'It won't be the same.'

'And I won't go blind.'

The threats must, I was sure, be pure hysteria and scare-mongering. For fear of law suits, perhaps, the risk had surely been grotesquely exaggerated for a neurotically safety-conscious society. If eclipses blinded their watchers, they would have names in folklore—the sight stealer, the blackness bringer, the melter of eyeballs. I had acquired a special lens, and said, 'Nor will I.'

Bill limped into the neighbouring house, and Fidelis said, 'He's decided to apply for Oxford. Not bad. Is that your phone ringing?'

I hadn't recognised the sound of my own mobile, brand newly acquired for taking with me to Portheglos. 'Mrs Merton? I have Mr Paxton for you.'

Mr Paxton wanted to read me a letter from Marguerite Lang's new solicitors. Not a very reputable firm, Paxton implied, ambulance chasers and corner cutters, and he guessed they were working for Mrs Lang on a contingent fee basis—a percentage of the profits or no fee at all.

I said, 'Oh dear,' and he replied:

'No, it's good news in a way, for the Kittermaster family, because it leads me to infer that she's less certain of her case than she's seemed so far. If there was no doubt as to her entitlement, why would she need other advisers?' I agreed that was one way of looking at it.

'Her real problem's proving the death of Justin Lang. I think we may have to concede he inherited on his mother's death, but Mrs Lang's got very little evidence of what happened to him.'

'She says he changed his name several times, and moved round the world, it might be difficult to find conclusive proof, but wouldn't that leave the estate in some kind of limbo?'

'The court would have to decide.'

'Just as a matter of curiosity, Mr Paxton—if Justin Lang were shown to have committed a serious crime . . .'

'Do you have a reason for asking that question, Mrs Merton?'

'No, it was just a thought. Sorry, do go on.'

He read me a formal demand that Mrs Marguerite Lang should be recognised as the rightful legatee of 447 Addison Road and all the goods and chattels therein that had pertained to the estate of Mrs Pearl Lang, and

232

the value, grossed up for inflation, of such items as had already, wrongfully, been sold. I asked what happened next, and Mr Paxton told me he'd spoken to the writer of the letter and been told that proceedings would commence as soon as Mrs Lang returned to London. I didn't know she'd gone away. 'Oh yes, she moved out of the Ritz with a companion. A young companion,' Mr Paxton said. 'An Australian known as Rick. They've gone on holiday, according to her new lawyer, though they couldn't go abroad.'

'Permit and visa problems?'

'Precisely. Now, Mrs Merton, there's something else, I had a call from your cousin Christina.'

'Yes?'

'She told me she's becoming very impatient to have everything settled.'

'Well, you knew that and so, my God, do I,' I said with feeling.

'She said something about taking matters into her own hands.'

'What did she mean by that?'

'I really couldn't say, but I thought perhaps you should be told, especially as I shall be on vacation for the rest of August. Tuscany.'

Skiing in February, Italy in summer—no doubt he'd be in the Caribbean for Christmas, I thought sourly, but said, 'I'm going to be away too, in Cornwall.'

'For the eclipse?' he asked. 'Won't it be

233

impossibly crowded? They say the population's going to be ten times its usual number. Rather you than me.'

Realising that every second of our conversation would be charged to the estate, I said goodbye without too many flowery compliments. While I'd been speaking Fidelis had fetched a pair of scissors and begun to dead-head faded roses from our boundary hedge.

'You don't usually garden, do you?' I asked.

'No, and I don't know how to either, but the contractor's missed a week so I'm filling in half an hour before my Hebrew lesson.'

'I wish I'd kept up with you, it's just I've had so much on.'

'Don't worry, everyone in Israel can speak English nowadays. Though I think they still have those intensive Hebrew courses for people who want to settle there.'

'I remember hearing they were quite strict about the language requirement for immigrants,' I said, distracted again by an unformulated thought. What was wrong with me this afternoon, why did I keep having ideas and failing to catch them? It was so hot. And the police business must have been more of a strain than I'd realised at the time. I'm not a reader of crime fact or fiction, I've never known why anyone finds violent death entertaining, and although I'd kept cool while talking to the officers and even Gayle, afterwards I'd felt sick and frightened at the thought of the battered, buried body. It was dreadful to imagine what had happened there. And why.

I said, 'Fidelis, can I ask you something?'

'Mm, of course—can you just hold on to this—oh, mind the thorns.'

I sucked blood from my finger. 'You once told me your own family perished during the war.'

'Well, I arrived on a children's transport in '39 and nobody ever turned up to claim me. Dresden, I came from. They could have died in the allied raids, the Dresden firestorm, but there's no record and it's much more likely they were in the camps, being Jews. I've always supposed they disappeared into that kind of darkness.'

The words chilled this peaceful summer afternoon, one on which women like me thought about making real lemonade and heard peaceful planes drone soothingly through the air. As incongruous to speak about death in a concentration camp, whether a German or a Japanese one, as it must have seemed in bourgeois Dresden before the Nazis, or, after the war, in Addison Road. 'Can I ask you something?' I said again.

'Something else?'

'If one of them turned up, Hitler or Mengele or Goebbels—any one of them, if they came near you now, if you could get near

235

one of them, what would you do?'

She stood still and silent for a while, the secateurs drooping in her hand. Then she snapped them viciously across a branch of buds and young blooms, and again. Psychiatrists always turn the question back to the questioner. 'What would you do yourself in the circumstances?' she said.

'I imagine I'd not dare to do anything. I'd not have the willpower.'

'I would.' Her voice was so cool that it took a moment for the incongruous words to settle on the soft air. 'If I could get my hands on the people who murdered my parents, I haven't the slightest doubt, I wouldn't have the slightest hesitation. I'd die myself, willingly, in taking their lives.'

At this moment Bill's music thudded out through the open windows next door. I couldn't put a name to the performer but the sound had become only too familiar, a strong, irregular beat with a plaintive, husky moan from an androgynous voice.

'You wouldn't bring the authorities into it, put them on trial? No legal retribution?'

'No. I'd kill.'

I didn't say any more, but went in to get cold drinks for us both. It took a bit of believing. After all these years, at her advanced age and with all her psychiatric experience, this orphaned human being still wanted revenge for the death of the mother and father she could not remember and believed that she herself, personally, would take it. But it made one wonder about Justin Lang. When he was told about the man who had tortured and killed his father (among so many other victims)—what would his reaction have been? I tried to summon up the image of the young man I remembered. Would he have killed?

CHAPTER TWENTY-EIGHT

e-mail to arilang@aol.com, sender hillyjames@ hotmail.com

Hi Ari, how R U? & for that matter where R U? I hope U'll get this message which I'm sending from Cape Town, as I told you I'm here with a tour group, thank your lucky stars you aren't along on this one (tho' it would be more fun for me to have you here) cos it's an unmixed party of wrinklies and crumblies and they all get lost and wander away and grumble because the weather's changed, been a pleasant winter up to now, and the trip was planned so as to be sunny but not hot but now it's raining and the pax seem to think it's all my fault. So it wasn't easy to escape, they obviously believe I'm paid to nanny them full time but after a week I said I was having an afternoon off and they'd have to like it or lump it, which is sure to mean complaints to my boss but it's just too bad and I'll take my chances.

So I went along to the address you said yr mother had sent you but nobody was in. It's a nice looking house, you might like going on a visit, there's a pool and a pretty garden. I met one of the neighbours, he said your mother went away suddenly after her friend that she looked after drowned in their pool. I was a bit surprised cos the way you talked about her, it sounded like your mother was the one that would need looking after, but apparently she was nursing her friend Mrs O'Riordan. Anyway, this man said he didn't have an address for your mother, though I expect she's been in touch with you herself by now, but an inquiry agent had been inquiring about her a couple of weeks ago and said there was a legacy involved and left an address here and the client's London number, 727 2644, so maybe you'll want to find out what that's about.

I'm doing two trips back to back, as soon as I've got this lot safely to Heathrow I've got to take an extra tour to Lithuania and Poland, it's a shame because it means it will be simply ages before we can meet but I'll keep in touch. Do let me know where your mother went, you've got me all curious now. Hope all's well, best wishes, Hilly x.

CHAPTER TWENTY-NINE

A clear sky was shining over the summer landscape of England as the crowded train hurtled westwards but the weather forecast was dire and the reserved though unoccupied seats showed how many people had been deterred by it. Nothing was going to put me off. I'd forced my way through the milling throng at Paddington, queued for the check-in and a boarding card never previously required for train travel, queued for a bike ticket and stood in another long line of people waiting to board the train.

Bored by an ill-chosen book, I picked up a discarded newspaper. Some ex-servicemen, now old men, claimed they had been subjected to tests of bacteriological weapons when stationed at Porton during their National Service in the 1950s. There had been deaths, there was subsequent, never explained, ill-health. Bertram's name was not mentioned. I turned to Katie's column. It began with an analysis of the eclipse's astrological significance. We could, it seemed, expect great consequences from the portentous conjunction of heavenly bodies. Reading on to the predictions I wondered whether Katie tailored them to suit herself and friends. Her own birthday was in December and I noticed she had told herself and other Capricorns, 'A white knight will come to your rescue this week.' What did she need rescuing from—Marguerite's demands? Her self-imposed attachment to the increasingly dismal house? Presumably it was with reference to that same quandary that I, a Virgo, was promised, 'A dramatic breakthrough is imminent, you can feel it in your bones.' I would have liked her to mean a breakthrough by the sun and moon of such clouds as might gather in the next forty-eight hours. But oddly enough, and annoyingly, given my scepticism about Katie's art, I did feel something in my bones. The excitement, of course, of seeing this long-desired phenomenon, but something else too, something I couldn't pin down, a kind of mixture of nervousness and foreboding—no, that's the wrong word. Expectation /anticipation. Something like that.

When I came over the last hill and freewheeled down towards Portheglos the sky was clear and the last of the day's sunshine lit up the cliffs that curled round the east side of the cove, leaving the rest in sharp shadow. For about two centuries, ever since the Romantics opened their eyes to the beauties of raw nature, unimproved/unspoilt/undeveloped landscapes such as this have seemed axiomatically beautiful. And of course Portheglos is beautiful by those standards, supremely so, but it doesn't move me nearly as

240

much as a scene rearranged by human hands. Give me the planned delights of Hyde Park any day; better still, the elegant vistas of built-up Bath or Edinburgh. True Kittermasters find their most sincere emotions aroused as they approach Portheglos. Not me.

The entrance to the estate was between a pair of lodges, each the holiday home of some cousin or another. I had never seen the double gates closed before. A huge new sign had been erected in front of the gates. It read 'Private Property. No entry, no camping, no stopping.' Big granite boulders lay on the grass verge, too close for a caravan or even a car to edge between them. Similar stones lined all the lay-bys on the road here from the station. Cornwall was repelling boarders.

Lookout Cottage was well placed for the evening sun. I found Katie sitting in its slanting rays, on a kitchen chair in the doorway, wrapped in a flowered apron and spotted headscarf, shelling large, old peas into a colander on her lap. I won't go so far as to say this tableau epitomised for me the generalised feeling of hostility with which I'd arrived, but it certainly sent through me a surge of irritation based loosely on the certainty that tough, maggoty home-grown vegetables, laboriously if virtuously prepared, are inferior in every respect but virtue to the shop-bought, frozen alternative. Convenience food and the Portheglos myth don't mix. This is the place

241

where working women become earth mothers and kids with an electronic lifestyle turn into characters out of Arthur Ransome or Enid Blyton. At this very moment, Katie told me, Christina was taking stuff down to the beach for a barbecue and her twins were collecting firewood with the gang. Torturing and competing with each other more like, I thought but didn't say.

'We've got a bit of a surprise for you, me and Christina.'

'Nice or nasty?' I asked nervously.

'Well, it might be a success, you must be longing to get things sorted too.'

'Katie, what have you done?'

'We decided to suggest meeting Marguerite out of London, everyone's always in a better temper here, the place works its magic—'

Not in my experience, I thought sourly.

'So we thought she could come here to supper tomorrow while you're still here.'

I hated the idea. That woman, on eclipse day. I won't be here, I thought, I'll leave before that, I'm not going to spoil the experience. I just won't. Failing to read my mind, Katie went on:

'We'll sit together like civilised women, without lawyers to interfere, and reach a sensible agreement about the house and the rest of the estate, we can't carry on in this strife and uncertainty and it's the perfect moment, the planets couldn't be more

242

propitiously disposed for bringing hearts and minds together, for all of us. You too, Vicky, your Luke's up with the band, you know.'

I didn't know. He hadn't told me. But he'd chosen to be here when there were so many other places he could have been, he had come to this place of bad memories where he knew I would be. My son had forgiven me. My heart singing, I watched a troop of about thirty children run down the slope, up and over the garden wall, across the grass, into the field and off out of sight. In front was a boy who might have been thirteen. Bringing up the rear were a couple of tots shouting, 'Wait for me.' The image was of Woodstock, flower-children and *fêtes-champêtres.*

'You see,' Katie said with a fond smile, 'everyone's having such fun, it's like a party all the time.'

I walked up the lane to the source of the loudest noise. Four young men were battering out a rhythmic cacophony. Others of their generation were lying on the ground around them, or jigging up and down in a kind of mild frenzy. I asked a harmless-looking girl if she'd seen Luke Merton, upon which she yelled, 'Lukie, over here!' and strolling out from a group of youths, came my son. The prodigal son? Or perhaps the prodigal mother. But we never attributed blame or expressed pleasure, Luke behaved as though we'd met on all our yesterdays and I followed his lead.

243

'Hi, Mum,' he said.

'Hi, Luke.'

'OK?'

'Fine, thanks, are you?'

'Great.'

'Got your eclipse viewer?'

'Yeah, yeah, don't fuss.'

'See you later then.'

That was the total conversation. We didn't touch or kiss or hug. But everything was all right again.

I was expected for drinks on Gayle's lawn and walked down towards her place realising there must be scores of people at Portheglos, perhaps even hundreds. Every house was bursting at the seams; every garden was full of tents and a communal marquee had been erected in the old paddock, containing trestle tables and benches, and a lot of draperies, and balloons, crates of fizzy drinks and cases full of baked beans. There were camp-fires in pits lined with flat stones and a home-made yurt lined with colourful kelims. There were kite-flying competitions and Ferdie Kittermaster-Matthews with his hang gliders. Two pop groups had come, one amateur and one professional (Georgie Kittermaster was the saxophonist) and an Irish cousin had brought her harp. I found Gayle in her element. Months previously she had hired a water bowser, now parked up by the first lodge, in case the mains supply failed, and a back-up electricity generator on wheels, ditto. She had installed a row of tall cubicles containing chemical toilets, a couple of Calor gas cookers and an industrial-size deep-freeze. Portheglos had been efficiently organised to withstand a siege. 'Nature intended you to be a lieutenant colonel,' I said and heard her younger cousin Mark mutter, 'Field marshal, more like.'

'The only problem is that I couldn't get them to block the coastal footpath, not even for a few days', Gayle said discontentedly. 'The county council really wasn't helpful at all, in spite of that awful map in the national papers that showed Portheglos as the best viewpoint of all. I really can't think how we can be sure everyone that's on the estate actually belongs here. I certainly don't know everyone else's guests if I see them.'

'She means there's a rival party going on up at the shooting butts and a beach barbie for the kids,' Mark explained. The shooting butts, at one time nothing more than man-height, had been built over the years into a rather tasteful studio used by a cousin who had become an installation artist. No doubt there was more noise and some illegal substances up there.

Gayle provided champagne, smoked salmon and Corelli on the sound system. She deployed her social skills, always seeming to know which people would already know each other and who didn't. I was introduced to the new au pair, who was a melancholy, bemused-looking Russian boy. I couldn't understand anything he said except when I asked how long he'd been here he replied, with the deepest gloom, three years. He wasn't doing very well in speech, though he seemed to take in what other people said. I was wondering why it's easier to understand a foreign language than express oneself in it, when my mind made a sideways leap and I suddenly thought, surely Marguerite should know Hebrew.

I remembered that day at the Ritz, when I'd gone there to speak to her, caught sight of her in the lobby and followed close behind her to the lift. The moment had been driven out of my head by shame and fury at her cruel description of me, but I remembered it now. There'd been a party of orthodox Jews going into the Marie Antoinette room, men in skull caps and women in evening dress, perhaps Israeli or perhaps British. Either way, they'd been speaking Hebrew. And one of them bumped into Marguerite and said something to her and she didn't understand. It was a foreign language to her.

But she'd told us she was a settler in Israel and produced the evidence of her marriage in Tel Aviv. The woman must have had to learn Hebrew. New immigrants underwent intensive language training, I knew that, so she'd certainly have taken in enough to understand if someone said sorry, or excuse me, or get out

246

of my way. Why had the phrase left her completely blank?

'Come on, Victoria, the midges are starting to bite, we're all going in.' Gayle's living-room was full of her usual, spectacular flower decorations; sent down from Pulbrook and Gould, she explained.

'What about supporting local industries then?' Mark asked nastily, and Gayle replied: 'They don't need little me, everyone's doing very nicely thank you out of this eclipse bonanza, traders are coining it what with pop festivals and people everywhere, the place is literally overrun.'

'I certainly passed a lot of new campsites on the way here,' I said.

'I shudder to think of the riff-raff flooding into the district, all those ravers and travellers. I think we should make a point of asking people who they are, if we don't recognise them.'

'That's everyone, is it, Gayle, all two million of them?' Mark said.

'Don't be silly, I mean anyone here, on the estate. Don't forget to keep an eye on anyone using the coastal footpath too, we've got to keep our eyes open.'

'Except when we're facing the sun.'

At this response, Gayle brought out a carton filled to overflowing with eclipse viewers, cardboard spectacle frames around sheets of mylar film, and began a speech about not looking at the sun with a naked eye. The conversation turned to pinholes in cardboard, reflections in buckets of water and various other old wives' tales.

I slid away, since I knew a good deal more than Gayle about viewing the eclipse and I had no intention of letting her bossy tones overshadow the occasion. I'd come to Portheglos in order to see the shadow of the moon sweeping at supersonic speed across the expanse of the sea. I was going to take up my position exactly in the place, obviously designed by nature as the perfect celestial viewing platform, from which I'd taken my first sighting of the stars, and heard of eclipses for the first time. The whole thing, as precise a manoeuvre for me as all Gayle's busybody arrangements for her entourage, had been my long-time plan. This was one of the few occasions in my hyper-cautious and pessimistic life, perhaps the only one ever, when I went to bed really, unreservedly, looking forward to something.

It was uncomfortable of course, but I felt a nervous agitation not simply due to the sleeping bag and blow-up mattress. Something was going to happen, something life-changing. Was seeing the total eclipse going to transform me into a different person? It was difficult to toss and turn because the mattress bounced me off it when I did, and I couldn't turn the light on to read, being on the floor of Katie's room. She'd have woken up and sympathised.

I used my usual insomniac's tricks to seduce sleep into taking me unawares. I thought about what I would see tomorrow. And even perhaps again—in Madagascar or Zimbabwe in 2001, or in Australia the year after that. If only I could have gone in previous years to New Guinea or India, to Hawaii, or the Philippines, to Winnipeg . . . what was it about those places that rang a bell when the boy Bill listed them?

The connection came to me as my mind dozily wandered, not with any surprise but as an obvious fact that I'd really always known, as immediately acceptable as any dream. These, of course, were the places Justin Lang had been seen in. Cousin Jeffrey mentioned some and others were named, though I didn't know what they were talking about at the time, by two unknown men at Bertram's funeral. *The chap was spotted,* one of them said, in Hawaii, in India. Of course he had been there. In all those places, the man who had so lightly inspired me with love for the stars and lust for a total eclipse had followed the phenomenon round the world himself. Actually, the total eclipse in Hawaii was in 1991, and Justin Lang was long dead by then, so there was a mistake somewhere but not one that worried my dozy, dormant brain.

I slept.

And woke to awful weather.

A sharp wind was rattling the doors in Lookout Cottage. Heavy white clouds scudded across a grey background. Katie was packing warm and waterproof gear before setting off to a prehistoric stone circle up on the moor. Incantations had been rehearsed and miracles were hoped for. Back lanes had been scouted out, to avoid the predicted gridlock.

'It's not actually raining,' Christina said.

'There's enough blue sky to make a sailor's trousers,' Katie said, pointing to a patch of broken cloud.

'It's moving, it'll break up by mid-morning,' Christina promised.

'It's coming from the west, it will have passed over by the time it matters,' Katie agreed.

Soon the full moon would slide its first tiny nick out of the western side of the sun. And behind the dismal cloud cover I couldn't even see where the sun was.

I moved away towards my pre-planned vantage point, on the cliff side of the garden wall. The daisies and ochre gorse bushes were tossing about in the gusty wind. The turf was short, welltrodden by enthusiasts who walk the coastal footpath. I spread my rug, unscrewed my vacuum flask and sat willing the sky to clear. The tide was going out. It would be low by noon.

Nine o'clock. First contact. But I couldn't see it.

People were making their way along the cliff edge, groups hunched into bright-coloured anoraks and fleeces, hunched under heavy rucksacks, coming out to see the wonder of the world. A family party, a jogger, an elderly couple in matching beige, a tall, bronzed man in a white T-shirt with a thin blonde woman wearing leather. With Marguerite Lang.

'Oh, Victoria, I wondered if we'd run into you, this is Rick.'

Rick, I recognised, had been the waiter in the Ritz Hotel, a friendly boy, less than half Marguerite's age.

'The girls were expecting you this evening,' I said. If she understood the sub-text, that she was unwelcome, that was fine by me.

'I know. We'll discuss my inheritance then, I think your cousins are beginning to see sense. But you aren't the only one who's interested in this eclipse, Victoria, I've always wanted to see it here.'

'I suppose Justin must have enthused about astronomy during your time together,' I said sourly, feeling a pang of jealousy. I didn't like the idea that my Star Man had been other people's also.

The sun was still obscured but the veil over it surely seemed to be just a little thinner. Just a little. Didn't it? If only I could have seen it there would be a curve of darkness cut out of the yellow disc.

I heard Christina calling, 'Come and watch

251

on TV, Vicky, there's a camera in an aeroplane above the clouds.'

I was damned if I'd sit indoors in front of a screen.

The grassy verge was filling up. People stationed themselves in a single row along the cliff top like a gaudy, badly drilled guard of honour. Walkers passed behind us, chattering, and I remembered Gayle's notion that every stranger should be challenged.

The sun must be more than half covered now, light beginning to diminish. But were the clouds just growing thicker?

'Look, there's a break coming,' Marguerite said. 'I'll see the eclipse at Portheglos yet.'

'You didn't say you'd been here before,' Rick said.

'I haven't, but I know lots about it. The famous family's famous bolt hole. I always wondered what it was really like.'

I thought of going somewhere else to get away from her, I couldn't have this moment desecrated, but Marguerite turned away saying, 'Justin didn't predict the weather when he told me Portheglos was right in totality's epicentre.' He'd told me that too. It's a date, he'd said.

'Come on, Rick, we'll get a better view out there on the point.'

Gently and inexorably it began to rain. Brightly striped umbrellas snapped open all round. I turned up my macintosh collar and knotted my spotted scarf more tightly round my neck.

This was the time when the western sky should darken, the blue sky—if only—should grow dull, the landscape take on a steel-grey, metallic sheen. The ground did glisten, as a matter of fact, but only on account of the blanketing damp. Ten forty-five. Fifteen minutes to go.

'There will be darkness visible,' a deep voice said beside me. A tall, burly man with wiry white curls bushing out from his head, his skin deeply tanned as though freckles had run together into a single coloration, his heavy-lidded, dark eyes weary and bloodshot, fixed on the horizon. Not dead, then; not forgotten. Here he was, punctually, in pole position. Where else should he be, but here where, decades ago, he'd foretold this numinous moment? With curious familiarity he put his hand, warm and heavy, on the small of my back. 'Wait,' he said.

And now the heartbreaking cloud didn't seem to matter. A huge circle of black darkness covered the sky overhead, an eerie orange glow illuminated all around its edges. Colour drained from the land and sea. Up the coast the town's lights snapped on. A flock of birds arrowed desperately to roost. The daisies in the hedge closed their petals tightly together. Everyone near by was awed into stillness and silence. The sun's loss struck terror into our hearts.

Then a pyrotechnic display of camera flashes went off all along the cliffs and fireworks were set off on the western headland, as, at the same moment, the church bells began to peal.

I heard nobody speak or move for an instant, or an eternity. And it was several minutes before the western sky began to brighten at the rim of the darkness. Invisible to anyone in this furthest, rain-sodden corner of Britain, a sliver of the crescent sun was emerging from the covering disc, and the dark shadow of the moon rushed off to the east. When I looked again at Justin Lang, there were tears in his eyes.

CHAPTER THIRTY

'Victoria! Vicky, where are you? Oh look, there she is.'

I didn't want to talk to anyone. Other people were moving away now, hunched against the rain. Gayle's brunch would be in full swing. The man I'd recognised after half a lifetime had remained about six feet away from me, standing still and thoughtful, moved, as I was, to a terror that felt as primitive and ancient as the planet itself. Seeing Justin, in this place, on this day, combined inevitability with amazement. Had he come because all

254

those years ago he'd said he would? But no; this was the only perfect viewing spot he could know of, in the narrow band of totality. Where else would he have gone?

Katie's voice came from just behind the grassy wall against which I was leaning.

'Vicky, here's someone needs to talk to you.' Perhaps it's Luke, I thought. 'Victoria!' she called again.

I turned. Katie, having pointed him in my direction, scuttled in out of the rain. I looked at the young man. Not Luke. Tall, European, but very dark of skin and hair and eye, angry-looking.

'Your neighbour in London said you'd be here,' he said. I looked at him blankly, half my mind still on what I'd just lived through. 'You were making inquiries about my mother.'

'Was I?' I asked vaguely.

'In Cape Town.'

'Oh yes. Marguerite.' I still wasn't quite with it and didn't really want to be. Who was this man? Why did he have to pester me now?

'There was something about a legacy.'

'Look, this isn't a very good moment, could you—'

'I need to find her.'

'Who are you?' I tried to pull myself together.

'My name's Ariel Lang.'

'You're Marguerite's son? She never mentioned having children.'

255

'Ariel!' Over a distance of thirty-eight years, I was familiar with this voice, last heard on this very spot. Justin Lang had turned towards the younger man. 'You are Ari?' he asked.

'Who are you?'

He can't have meant the question. When they were face to face the likeness between the two men was unmistakable. The eclipse had united them as it had Luke and me—but after how long? 'I don't know you', the younger man said. I realised my own hand had gone to my own heart. If Luke had said that to me . . . !

'My son!'

'You,' the young man said. 'It's been too long. It's too late. What are you doing here?'

Justin replied in Hebrew. He held his strong arms out towards his son with undisguised emotion. His son, I thought, Marguerite's son, how extraordinary. But whether it was hate-filled or loving, this was not a reunion a stranger ought to watch. The emotions were too personal and too raw. I turned my face away and strolled a little distance with mock carelessness. (Much later you told me my incuriosity made me unique among women, but I wasn't incurious, only respectful of your privacy. I couldn't have borne to be seen if Luke spurned me.)

I looked down over the cliff edge. The tide was almost fully out so the sand and rocks of the enclosed beach were exposed and I could see children and their parents cooking up on

256

their driftwood fire in spite of the rain. The smell of burnt sausages drifted up towards me. Immediately below where I was standing on the cliff edge fierce breakers were splashing on the rocks. A lighter shade of grey showed stones which the sea never reached.

Then I saw Marguerite and her Rick rounding the corner and turning back on to the cliff path, coming towards me. Her leather trousers and jacket, soaked through, clung to her lean limbs and blonde dreadlocks tossed under the brim of a rain-sodden hat. She could have been Rick's grandmother at that moment, but he still held her arm like a courtly gallant.

It's like a play I thought, though I wasn't sure if it was a classical tragedy reuniting parent and long-lost child, or an implausible Whitehall farce, as the dramatis personae popped back from the dead. But Justin wasn't dead, and it came to me that Marguerite always knew that. She just believed she'd get away with saying he was. Well, if I'd been married to that woman I'd have dropped out of her life myself. Not out of my son's, though, not if I could help it.

Marguerite's eyes fell on the young man and passed indifferently on. He saw her, and didn't react either. It wasn't possible, I thought, fresh from yesterday's encounter with Luke. Hostility or jealousy or love or disgust—there had to be some recognition and emotion

257

between mother and son. Or was she protecting herself from pain, as I might have done any time in the last two years, if I'd run into Luke by accident knowing he'd repudiated me. I couldn't let him do it to her, never mind disliking her, this was more than even she deserved.

'Ariel,' I called. 'Ariel, aren't you going to say hullo to your mother?'

He didn't come towards her or hold out his arms, any more than he had to Justin. A dysfunctional family, I thought in modish jargon, and then corrected myself: a tragic family. Ariel stared with an icy chill in his eyes and then he said:

'That's not my mother.'

I emitted a manic giggle, thinking, I don't believe this. But what could one say? That she wasn't at her best, or she looked thirty years older with all the cosmetics washed off? They confronted one another, there on the cliff. Marguerite opened her mouth to speak when Justin laughed, a deep, pleasant sound and said:

'It's little Marlene, after all these years— how've you been doing?'

She paled, then flushed scarlet. 'Who's that? Justin? Justin Lang! Oh my God, I can't believe it, she said you were dead—wild horses wouldn't have got anything about the murder out of me if I'd had any idea . . .'

Ari pushed his face between them, towards

258

the woman who wasn't his mother, and hissed, 'Who are you?'

And I said stupidly, 'You mean you're not Justin's wife?'

'Of course she isn't poor Emm,' Justin said.

'What have you done to her?' Ari shouted. 'Where's my mother?'

'But who's Marguerite then?' I asked.

And Justin responded, 'This is Marlene from the old days at Addison Road.'

'Mrs Beak's granddaughter? That Marlene? No wonder you knew your way round the house,' I realised.

'You told me about eclipses,' she said to Justin, and the same pang of irrational jealousy struck me again.

'What are you doing here?' Ari shouted, as I stumbled on:

'But I don't understand. If you're not Marguerite what gave you the right to—'

She interrupted angrily. 'Rights, is it? So what gives you rights, you and your precious cousins? Some God-given rule that means you get to hold on to all this and me and my gran go on servicing the likes of you?'

'You must be Lenny, you were the hairdresser,' I murmured.

'My mother's hairdresser? What is this? Answer me!'

'So what if I was a hairdresser? I've done my share of scraping a living, servicing all the rich bitches in the world, yes, your precious mother too, whining old woman that she was, it's my turn now.'

'You met Emm Lang in hospital, you chummed up with her,' I said.

'I know about you, you're the woman that took her away to Cape Town, her carer, she depended on you!' Ari accused.

'Wouldn't have done her much good depending on you instead, would it?' she jeered. 'You were far too busy for a useless old woman. Postcards and not that many of them, that was all you were ever good for that I remember. She kissed them, d'you know that? Slobbered her kisses on to pointless pictures 'cos you'd scribbled your name on the back. Some son you turned out to be.'

'And you realised you knew her husband,' I said slowly. 'You remembered him!'

'She thought you were long since dead.' Marguerite/Marlene said to Justin.

'So now she's dead instead,' Ari shouted. He was blazing with anger, though, I realised later, it was directed at himself. He'd neglected his mother.

'D'you care?' Marguerite—no, Marlene—asked. 'Like you ever came to see her yourself? Like you gave a flying fuck what happened to her? She'd talk about her boy Ari this and Ari that and at the end she sometimes thought you were actually there but you weren't, Ari, were you, she didn't matter, she was just a poor old bag with Alzheimer's to you, 'cos you'd no idea she could have been a millionaire, she never even knew it herself so why should she have the benefit of it?'

'Millionaire?' he muttered.

'Don't you wish you'd known about that? But not you, not her either, it was me, Lenny O'Riordan, not mad old Emm, me that read about the old Kittermasters dying, me that knew who owned the London house, me that read what it's worth. And me that saw you that night, Justin, back in 1961, you and the famous saintly Bertram dragging a body along the road. Oh yes, you can look surprised but I did see you, I really did. OK, so maybe I never understood what was happening, and when nothing was ever said I forgot all about it. But when they found the body it was in the papers, and I knew then all right. You owe me.'

'So you stole my mother's name, did you kill her too, did you push her wheelchair into the pool?' Ari shouted.

I don't think Ari meant to do the woman actual harm. I really don't think so. But in stepping forward towards her, his face contorted in a mask of fury, he caused her to back away from him. It was unintentional, it must have been, but the grass was slippery and there was no fence.

'Marguerite!' I shrieked at the same moment that Justin roared, 'Marlene, take care!' and Rick, who'd been listening with a blank, bemused expression on his handsome

261

face, shouted, 'Hey, look out' and grabbed at her arm.

Marguerite slid backwards. For a moment it seemed all right, it wasn't a disaster, her legs were dangling in the air but her body was firmly pressed on the cliff-top grass. But at the very moment that Rick grasped her hand, her chest slipped further downwards. For what felt like eternity, she stayed there halted between safety and death.

'Come on, easy now, we'll haul you up,' Rick said, and Ari and Justin jostled to lean over to reach for her other hand. Then she screamed, a piercing, lingering terror, as the soil of the sodden cliff top gave way, her wet wrist slipped through Rick's wet palm, and she slipped, slid, tumbled straight over the cliff. The awful sound stayed in my ears long after it stopped and there was no real noise but the thundering waves.

I saw her collapsed on the jagged rocks below with her straggling hair like a sea anemone in a rock pool and a great patch of red spreading in the water. The waves quickly dragged and tossed her into the grey sea but something must have caught on a rock because the body was stuck, tugged to and fro but never freed to be carried out to sea. Nobody could climb down there or reach the spot from the beach. It was inaccessible. After the rescue helicopter came they said she must have died at the moment of impact. I hope it was true.

CHAPTER THIRTY-ONE

The day after Justin Lang came back into my life his name came into public awareness. The police did a press release on 'The Body in the Bomb Site'. It didn't make headlines because most space was occupied with a post-mortem on the eclipse, of which, I bitterly realised, I would have seen far more if I'd stayed at home in Hampstead. There were lots of tales of downpours throughout the West Country, Dunkirk spirit in Cornish holiday resorts and bankruptcy for the organisers of pop festivals. Over eighteen months the progression had been from Hope through Hype to Recrimination. Even the ever self-confident Gayle was kicking herself for having made what now seemed to be hysterical preparations. But that was a brief and uncharacteristic moment of self-blame, banished by self-righteous fury when she saw the story. There was the Kittermaster name, and there was the accusation of murder. For her, a disaster. For Justin, a warning to do again what he'd done in 1961 and leave the country. Only this time he didn't take dangerous information with him. He took me.

*　　　*　　　*

Justin told me the police had got the outline of the story right. The victim was the man known as Dr Tomo Matsuzakara and his American passport did say he was a businessman and he was connected with the house in Addison Road. Inspector Strange admitted that there'd been an anonymous letter saying so, after the body was found and mentioned in the press.

'That must have been Marguerite, I mean Marlene,' I realised. 'But how did she know?'

'She was always following me around, that girl, she had a real crush on me,' he said. And another time I heard about her ambition, her jealousy. She was always greedily fascinated by the Kittermasters and wanted everything they had for herself. I couldn't blame her for that.

You told me about that night. For anyone else reading this account (though it's for you, my love, that I've written it) this is what Justin said happened:

'Bertram rang and summoned me to the house. I didn't want to go, it was the climbing season and I'd booked a weekend on Snowdon, but he'd never asked anything of me before. We weren't close, but he'd always treated me fairly and I respected him. So I went round on the Friday. Elena and the girls were down in Cornwall, nobody else was in the house. Dreary place, I never liked it, Bertram was welcome to stay there. I cooked him a fry-up because he couldn't have made so much as a cup of tea for himself, and he told me he'd

264

seen Saburo Okuda. I did know what Bertram's research was about, bacteriological weapons, but I knew very little else about it except that my father had been a victim of Japanese experiments, so at first I didn't know what he was talking about.'

'Your father—'

'I don't remember him, he died in a concentration camp in Manchuria sometime during the war. And after the war some of the worst of the Japanese, the ones who'd conducted the most cruel experiments, they were given new identities and taken to America.'

'That's unbelievable!' I cried.

'Believe me, there's little room for moral considerations in warfare, I've had ample opportunity to find that out since. This was the height of the Cold War and they'd rescued some of the worst German scientists too, because the struggle against the Soviets outweighed any moral considerations. So in 1961 when Bertram went on an official visit to one of the American labs, he was introduced to Dr Matsuzakara and recognised him as Dr Saburo Okuda whom he'd met thirty years earlier. The man who'd been second-in-command at Pingfan. A war criminal, one of the vilest men ever to live. My father's murderer.'

'What happened?'

'Okuda was being sent to Porton. Bertram

felt he had to tell me—really, I think, he needed to get it off his chest and who else could he tell? We spent the whole of that afternoon talking and arguing, we went to the river and along the embankment, miles we walked that day. Bertram was usually a decisive man, not one for crises of conscience, still less one who needed validation of his actions, but I don't remember which of us suggested it first, and it doesn't matter. Bertram invited the man to dinner on the way through London, that was the next day, Saturday. And when he came to the house I killed him.'

'Justin! How?'

'It was primitive. I've learnt sophistication since. I coshed him with a brick in a sock, if you want to know, and then I burnt the sock in the Aga. He was a little, thin man, you wouldn't have guessed his history from looking at him. It was so easy. We crammed the body into the little girls' twin-pram, a hulking great coach-built thing, and pushed it up the road. I've taken lives since then and been more frightened but I'll never forget that evening. Howling gale blowing, pouring with rain. At least it meant we didn't meet anyone in the street. We went as far as the bomb site where they were building a new housing estate and then we buried it. I saw them pouring concrete over the very place the next day.'

'And Marlene must have been sneaking

266

along behind.'

I could see the tall, blonde teenager, plump because her staple diet would have been fish and chips and spotty because working-class children didn't eat much fruit in those days. Dazzled by the glamorous Justin who had bothered to notice her, talking to her about politics and astronomy. He'd made her feel special. She'd have gladly gone to work with her gran in the hope of seeing him. I expect she'd wait in the street near his flat at weekends to catch sight of him. There, outside the house in Addison Road, that Saturday night, hovering in the shadow of a garden wall and waiting for him to come out and turn up the dark street towards the Tube station so that she could meet him 'by accident'. And then, instead, the two men, her hero and his famous stepfather, and their incomprehensible burden. An unfading memory for both of them, though in Marlene's, Lenny's, or (as we later discovered she always spelt the name) Leni's, the image probably dwindled until it seemed no more real to her than a movie she'd once seen, or a dream. Maybe she'd never understood what happened until all those years later when she read about the body found in the exact spot where she'd seen the two men digging.

If they thought nobody had seen them, why did Justin have to disappear?

'I'd been meaning to go in any case, I'd

267

been talking about it and putting it off for years. I was a firm Zionist at the time. And Bertram wanted the Israelis to be warned about the biological weapons they were developing, all in the name of defence. He said there'd been Egyptian scientists where he went in America, and Syrians too, but no Jews. Israel was hideously vulnerable and surrounded by enemies looking for ways to destroy it.'

'Bertram wasn't Jewish himself, was he?'

'No, but he loved Pearl. He knew she was still in love with my father and still married to him, but he was willing to go through a form of marriage to rescue her. Bertram was glad of any affection she could spare him, he told me once.'

'Poor Elena, I think she always sensed that.'

'Yes, I don't think Bertram could ever forget his feelings for Pearl.'

'And the house was really hers?'

'She brought her own father's collection of chinoiserie to England, it was worth a lot of money even then. So she bought the house and hoped against hope for my father to escape and get out of China and join us one day. She did it for my sake, you know. If it hadn't been for me she'd never have left him behind.'

'And it was for her sake that Bertram passed secrets to Israel?'

'He was too much of a scientist for such personal considerations, he did it because he knew it was right.'

Taking with him a file of secret papers and his stepfather's blessing,. Justin had left for Israel the next day. I don't think the kibbutz he first lived in can have felt any more strange to the Anglicised public-schoolboy Justin than Haifa does now to me.

Justin, or Yossi Yadin as he's called now, met Emmi, formerly Marguerite, in the kibbutz to which, as new settlers, they had both been assigned. Even when they were still officially together, they led an oddly disconnected life, for the movements of a spy are inevitably erratic. Once in the Israeli secret service, always in it and always secretive. So he's not told me anything about that side of his career. I do know he's been a climber and used to meet Bertram in the mountains from time to time. They kept in touch, though Elena never knew of it. And he's an astronomer, discovered a comet, named a newly found star after his mother—Pearl Lang twinkles eternally in a distant galaxy—and collected every total eclipse since the Winnipeg one in 1979. He's taken me to an all-night meteor-shower party in the desert and next year, in 2001, we shall see the total eclipse under the clear skies of East Africa, choosing, as we both did in Cornwall, the perfect viewing spot in the small area where absolute totality can be observed.

I'm enjoying the freedom of life as a

stranger in a strange land. Actually the Mount Carmel district, where Yossi and I live, has certain similarities to Hampstead where I have kept my flat on, and sometimes stay with Luke who is living in it. Last time I was in London I went past 447 Addison Road. Spruced up and revamped, it looks worth every penny of the five million pounds its buyer paid. Under the firm guidance of Mr Paxton a division of the spoils was agreed. Katie used her third share to buy a house on a ley-line not far from Portheglos where she runs residential courses in astrology and 'earth mysteries': Christina put all of hers into a five-storey house in Notting Hill. Ari used the money his father disclaimed to move to California with a sweet, soft-skinned convert to Judaism called Hilly. He does research into Jewish history. She intends to devote herself to producing grandchildren for Yossi, one a year, like an orthodox bride.

I started out in life all over again in my fifty-first year. I've been liberated by leaving England, or perhaps it was you that did that; Yossi/Justin, the man of my dreams. Many the inhibition I've abandoned, as you so intimately know, and as I was reminded by Fidelis's obvious amusement on my last trip to London, when I argued with a taxi driver, shouted at one of the boys next door and told Gayle to get stuffed when she rang, as she does every time she hears I'm back, to ask the same old questions. She's determined to get to the bottom of what happened at Portheglos on the day of the eclipse, and wants an explanation of events in Addison Road in 1961. She has guessed I know more than I'm telling about the Japanese corpse and the Kittermaster connection and the last time we spoke she accused me of shielding a murderer. I'm not sure whether she meant Marlene's killer—the verdict was accidental death—or Dr Tomo Matsuzakara's. She couldn't have been talking about poor Emm's, though the more I think about its timing the more likely it seems that she was pushed into the swimming pool to drown. Nor did Gayle mean the mass murder of thousands of Matsuzakara/Okuda's innocent victims.

I'm not going to tell her she's right. But of course I really am shielding a murderer, because I am sure that the revered Bertram Kittermaster and his stepson Justin Lang took an entirely justified revenge.

You wiped a monster from the face of the earth. Was that a crime?

We hope you have enjoyed this Large Print book. Other Chivers Press or Thorndike Press Large Print books are available at your library or directly from the publishers.

For more information about current and forthcoming titles, please call or write, without obligation, to:

Chivers Press Limited
Windsor Bridge Road
Bath BA2 3AX
England
Tel. (01225) 335336

OR

Thorndike Press
P.O. Box 159
Thorndike, Maine 04986
USA
Tel. (800) 223-2336

All our Large Print titles are designed for easy reading, and all our books are made to last.